PLAYING IN THE DARK

playing in the dark

A NOVEL BY

KENT THOMPSON

QUARRY PRESS

The publisher thanks the Ontario Arts Council and The Canada
Council for assistance in publishing this book.

CANADIAN CATALOGUING IN PUBLICATION DATA

Thompson, Kent, 1936–
  Playing in the dark

ISBN 0-919627-83-8

1.Title.

PS8589.H5P43 1990   C813'.54   C90-090164-0
PR9199.3.T46P43 1990

Design and imaging by ECW Type & Art, Oakville, Ontario.
Printed and bound in Canada by Hignell Printing Limited,
Winnipeg, Manitoba.

Distributed in Canada by University of Toronto Press,
5201 Dufferin Street, Downsview, Ontario M3H 5T8 and in the
United States of America by Bookslinger, 502 North Prior Avenue,
St. Paul, Minnesota 55104.

Published by Quarry Press Inc., P.O. Box 1061, Kingston,
Ontario K7L 4Y5 and P.O. Box 348, Clayton, New York 13624.

. . . when a crime has been committed, the victim has a fact — the crime — to which to respond. The law defines a wrong. But when no crime has been committed, although one was intended, the victim must respond to what might be termed an *unconsummated crime*, and the response must necessarily be uncertain, uneasy — and, insofar as the victim is concerned — unending. It cannot be put right, as a crime is, by punishment. The victim must seek other forms of justice . . . .

— T.L. Beckwith, *When the Law Fails*

I

You could smell the drink on him when he entered the bank, he was dirty, his clothes were dirty. We left a space around him; we didn't want to look at him. His face was grimy, his long fair hair was greasy, one arm was smeared with a blue tattoo, he was wearing dirty yellow gloves, he was still drunk. It was a snake tattoo.

When his turn came he did not go to the next available teller, as he should have, but went instead to Sharon Branaman's station, where the little sign indicated that her position was closed and that customers should go to the next station. Sharon was counting money; she was going to open in five minutes. He took off one of his gloves; he handed the note to her.

She read the note and took it to Mrs. Purvis. As she did so, the young man went to the gate that separated the front of the bank from the working area, reached over, and unlatched the barrier. He was pointing a finger at Mrs. Purvis when she read the note and looked up at him, puzzled. She was an older woman — square and solid, proud of her long brown hair, her crowning glory, a gift from God. She had a husband and two grown sons. She had worked for the bank for 19 years. She said: "I don't have the key."

He yelled at her. "Yes you do, god-damn you, you do!"

Then he grabbed her hair with both his hands and used it to pound her head on the desk. He knocked a tooth out; there was blood everywhere. The bank was silent except for the thud, thud.

He turned and ran out the door of the bank, which hissed slowly closed.

2

Sharon explained to her mother that the first concern of everyone in the bank was for Mrs. Purvis. They didn't even notice the fellow running away, and no one cared about the note, which fell on the floor and wasn't found until the police hunted for it, hours later. At the time everyone in the bank was concerned for Anne Purvis. Not only had she lost a front tooth, but her nose was smashed, both her eyes blackened, and she had bitten off a piece of her tongue. The blotter beneath her head was saturated with blood. She was unconscious, and the first thing they did was call for an ambulance. It was only when the ambulance was on its way that the bank manager thought to call the police. By that time, Sharon explained, the man could have been half-way to Montreal.

"What did the note say?" her mother asked. They were in the dining room, where they did their ironing. They might have used another room. There were empty rooms on the third floor, but they used the dining room. Her mother was ironing Sharon's yellow dress. Sharon was dark, and looked good in yellow.

"I don't remember exactly," said Sharon. " '*Give me all the money in the vault,*' or something like that."

Sharon fetched and added two more summer dresses to the pile of her mother's ironing. Sharon admitted that she hated ironing; she would be happy to do some other job around the house if only her mother would iron for her. Her mother agreed to the idea — but, she said, Sharon might clean the house once a week. She repeated *once a week*. This agreement had been made a long time ago. Sharon said she would do her best, but reminded her

8

mother that it was a big house — must she clean the third floor? (No, the third floor did not have to be cleaned every week — just every so often, that would do, when it needed it.) It seemed sometimes that her mother forgot she had a full time job, *too*.

Sharon had worked at the bank for almost three years now. After high school she had gone to the university — which was right there, handy — for a year, but didn't find it very exciting, and when the opportunity presented itself to work in the bank, she took it until something more interesting turned up.

"The worst of it," she told her mother, "is that I think I recognized the guy. He's the guy who's been following me around town for the past few weeks."

"Is that true?"

"Yes!" said Sharon.

"Well," said her mother — and then pointing to the yellow dress on the ironing-board — "What did you spill on this?"

"I don't know," said Sharon. "Ice cream, probably."

"I wish you'd wash the spots out first instead of relying on the washing machine to do it. You ask too much of the washing machine."

"We need a new washing machine."

"I don't think we can afford one," her mother said.

Sharon made a face to indicate that she'd heard that before. Her mother had a good job — she worked in administration up at the hospital. They didn't have any debts, so far as Sharon knew. The house was paid for. She was sure of that.

"It doesn't matter," said Sharon, referring to the dress.

"I think it does," said her mother. Her mother was tenacious. Everyone said that about her. And if Sharon had told her mother that she was considered *tenacious*, her mother would have been proud of it.

9

"It's my dress," said Sharon. "You worry too much."

"Yes," said her mother sharply, "and you're the cause of most of it."

The discussion felt all too familiar.

"Did you tell the police about this fellow following you?"

"No," said Sharon. "Not yet."

"Well you *should*!" said her mother. "Why didn't you tell them you thought he was the fellow who had been following you when you talked to them yesterday?"

"I didn't think of it," said Sharon. "They didn't ask."

Her mother looked at her with suspicion. She didn't even attempt to conceal her doubt.

"We're going to have an argument if we're not careful," said Sharon. "I'm going out."

"I thought you were going to clean the house."

"I said I'd clean the house just as soon as it needed it."

"You don't think it needs it?"

"No," said Sharon, gesturing around. "It looks fine."

"Does that include your room?"

"My room is fine."

"I'm sure it is."

"What do you mean by that?" said Sharon.

"I'm sure your room is neat and clean," said her mother.

"It's my room," said Sharon. "Have you been going into my room?"

"For heaven's sake, Sharon," said her mother. "We *both* live here."

"You stay out of my room," said Sharon. "I'm going out."

"What about that fellow you say is following you?"

"Well," said Sharon, "if he kills me, it's your fault, isn't it."

She left before her mother could argue further.

3

Nobody could say that it wasn't a large house. The word most easily applied to it was *spacious*. They didn't even use the third floor which, when the house was built shortly before the Great War, was designed to provide living quarters for three servants. But there had never been any servants. Life had changed just about then. The Branaman family decided to employ a "daily."

Not that the family was suddenly poor. The great-grand-father who had the house built was a provincial court judge, and Lee Branaman's father (Sharon's grandfather) was a prominent lawyer, well-connected politically. You just couldn't get servants then.

A central feature of the house was the large study on the ground floor, the walls lined with law books and, in the center, a massive desk with a small brass lamp with a green glass shade. Sharon loved that lamp when she was a little girl. She ran her fingers over it — only when she was alone in there, of course: she'd been told not to touch it.

"Why *not*?"

"You're too young."

Along the front and side of the house was a wide veran-dah — a nice place to sit on summer evenings. It caught the breeze. There was a swing on the verandah, and on warm evenings she and her father sat on the swing and he read to her while, with his toe on the floor, he urged the swing back and forth.

"Stop it!" she cried. Did he want her to upchuck?

He laughed. Where did she learn that word — *upchuck*?

"I found it in my tummy," she said, and he laughed again. She was pleased; she had pleased him very much.

The ground floor had an entrance hall and a living room on the right as you entered — just across the hall from the study. Behind the living room was the dining room, and behind that the kitchen.

A broad stairway rose from the wide front hallway, and upstairs on the left (as you ascended) was the master bedroom, which ran nearly the length of the house, and on the right, two bedrooms, one to the front of the house and one to the rear. The one to the rear was Sharon's, and always had been. Across the hall from it was the stairway to the third floor (there was a plain wooden door; it was closed) and the bathroom. There was a door from the master bedroom to the bathroom and another to the hall — but her parents had direct access to the bathroom, and that sometimes meant that Sharon was left jumping up and down outside the bathroom door and stamping her feet while her father laughed and teased her from inside.

Her father was not a lawyer. He was an elementary-school teacher. People who knew the family sometimes remarked that this was something of a come down, wasn't it? But then Lee Branaman had always been a bit of an odd duck, and careless. It was a strange word to use: *careless*. There was the time he decided to try a paper route and then decided he didn't like it — but didn't bother to tell anyone. No one in the neighborhood got their papers for a week, and there was a soggy pile of bundled newspapers on the Branaman's front lawn until someone figured out the problem.

He met Lorraine Ashton when she was a student nurse at the Victoria Public Hospital and he was a patient there, having his appendix removed. He was twenty one, and just completing his course at the Normal School. She dropped out of nurses' training to marry him.

He taught in a small school in the eastern part of the province for two years but moved back to stay with his mother when his father died. There was plenty of room in the house. Sharon was born just after his mother died — so Sharon had grown up in the large house, and bitterly resented her mother's recent suggestion that they might move into an apartment. "This is *my* house as much as it's yours!" she cried.

After Sharon went out (not saying where she was going, of course), Lorraine ironed the two dresses and then gave the house a quick vacuuming. She especially resented vacuuming the stairs; it meant lugging the upright vacuum cleaner up one step at a time, wrestling it back and forth. The attachments didn't do the job they were supposed to do; they never did. And she was tired. She would be tired at work the next day, which irritated her. She would probably say something silly and the Administrator would speak to her with infuriating patience.

She did not go into Sharon's room.

What made her angry, she said, was not cleaning the house, but that Sharon so easily neglected their agreement. It wasn't as if Sharon were a child anymore. They were two grown women sharing a house, and it wasn't fair.

But Sharon apologized as soon as she was in the door, and admitted that her mother was right. She did not know why she was so unreasonable. She guessed she was just feeling restless. And she hadn't done anything exciting that evening. She and some of the girls from the bank had gone to a movie — a very boring movie, not worth talking about — and then walked through the Mall. "I think I saw the guy who robbed the bank," she said. "Up at the Mall. I think he was following me."

"For heaven's sake, call the Police. Right now!"

Sharon shrugged. "I'm not *positive*," she said. "You don't want me to make a fool of myself, do you?"

Lorraine was exhausted. She just couldn't deal with her much more. Lorraine felt as if every bone in her body had melted.

4

That night Lorraine heard Sharon wandering around the house. It was something to which Lorraine had never become accustomed, although it seemed like Sharon had always done it — which seemed to Sharon sufficient reason to continue. She said that: "I've *always* done it." As a little girl she often got out of her bed and padded downstairs in her jammies to visit her father in the study. He was a night-owl, too. He liked to sit at his father's desk in the study and have a last drink or two.

Lorraine remarked that people would think it very odd indeed if they knew that their Grade Seven teacher drank Scotch. People wouldn't like to think so.

Lee agreed that it was probably pretty odd.

Sharon sat on his lap and sometimes fell asleep there. Lorraine found herself impatient with Lee, and more than once she·marched down to ask him to please come to bed, and he said he would, in a minute, he just wanted to finish his drink. But he'd pour himself another, she could hear him, and by the time he got up to the bedroom after carrying Sharon to her room, Lorraine was irritable, cold, and resentful.

And after he left them, one of the things Sharon did, and was doing now, was go through the kitchen and dining room, banging the cupboard doors — probably just to annoy her mother. Lorraine asked her in the morning if she found what she was looking for — and Sharon replied that she was looking for something to do, was there anything wrong with that? She was bored. "I try to be quiet," she said, "and I don't even turn on the lights."

And now this story about being followed by the fellow

who robbed the bank. It was quite surprising, really, that they hadn't caught him yet. Gossip up at the hospital (which the ambulance drivers picked up from the police) was that the police knew who he was and that it was only a matter of time until they picked him up. The police weren't in any great panic because he didn't get any money in the robbery and Mrs. Purvis seemed to be recovering quite well. Her injuries were temporarily disfiguring, but superficial. She didn't much like to have visitors because she looked so awful and couldn't talk at all because of the missing tooth and swollen tongue, but those things could be fixed. Both her sons came up from Saint John to visit her and brought her stuffed toys — a stuffed pink rabbit and a large black bear. It was apparently a family joke because Anne Purvis laughed so hard she almost fell out of bed. The nurses remarked that you never knew, did you. You thought somebody was just kind of quiet and ordinary — and all of a sudden you find out these secrets.

The bank manager came to visit, and several of the tellers. Sharon did not visit. She had never liked the hospital much, and even as a little girl didn't want to go there to visit her mother at work. She'd only been there once, with a severe earache. Besides there was no point in lying about it — she didn't think Anne Purvis was the greatest person in the world. "She could be very bossy, and she was a prude," said Sharon.

Nor was Sharon overly impressed by the information that her mother got from the ambulance drivers about the bank robber. It seemed he was a local boy who grew up in Gibby's Junkyard just outside town. Nobody knew if Gibby was the guy's father or not. His mother was supposed to have been Rosie Keeler, who left town some years ago, nobody knew where. People talked about her as *mean*. She'd do anything she felt like doing. You couldn't get a thing out of her. She said "shit in my hat, shit in my hat" in response to almost everything. She'd been staying with Gibby before and after she was arrested for shoplifting. Nobody knew if she had the boy with her when she arrived in town or if she had him while she was here and left him with Gibby, and no one, for various good reasons, wanted to ask Gibby. So the kid had grown up among wrecked cars, broken glass, rusting parts, old grease, empty whiskey bottles, and the usual series of mean mongrel dogs. "You know what they say about junkyard dogs?" said the ambulance driver. "Well, it's all true. Take your leg off if Gibby isn't standing right there."

The kid had apparently gone out West for a while — got into trouble, and did time in Kingston for armed robbery. Not a nice place at all. He came home tattooed all over — but not prison tattoos. Artist work. The police said he had a snake coiled around his arm that looked at you. It was the only scary thing about him. They weren't surprised he'd botched the robbery. "These guys," they said, "talk tough, but when they go into action they're usually too drunk to do it well. The public should be grateful for booze. Without it, some of these guys would be a real problem."

Sharon said the guy probably went to school with her. He was probably in her Daddy's class. She wondered why he looked so familiar.

5

Lorraine admitted it freely enough — she was a dry stick of a woman, usually. Her nursing classmates said of her that she was too serious, took things too hard, and they were surprised that she didn't do better on the quizzes: they didn't think they were too hard, and she was so *serious*. Example: one night in the student nurses' residence they all stayed up late memorizing the nervous system, using all the usual mnemonic verses and giggling, running to the bathroom, all of them quite scatty. Girls get like that. Somebody opened a door and popped into Lorraine's room — hiding from another girl — and Lorraine looked up from her desk. "Please," she said. "Oh please." She looked stricken, heartbroken.

When Lee (he was a patient, so this was all quite forbidden) made his move — he took her hand, quite properly, and quite improperly kissed it, gazing up at her — she thought she would die. Oh, she went quite mad then. Clothes, perfume, laughter — and she failed three quizzes in a row; the other girls thought she was cracking up and held impromptu conferences about her and wondered if they shouldn't speak to the Director of Nursing Studies about her, but didn't.

Then Lee was discharged and went away and didn't call and Lorraine tried desperately to make up for lost time, but she fainted in the operating room during an appendectomy. There was a talk with the Director of Nursing Studies, and she was asked to leave.

6

Lorraine did not call the police when Lee disappeared. She told herself that she was too stunned, too surprised. It never occurred to her that the police might be interested. She did not even admit to the school authorities that Lee was gone until he had missed over a week of teaching and the principal was saying to Sharon that he hoped her father was feeling better. Sharon came home and attacked her mother: *where was he?*

The police, Lorraine reasoned, would want to know things that were none of their business. There was no crime involved, was there?

There was nothing *wrong*. She defied anyone to say there was anything *wrong*. There was nothing wrong except the usual, normal disagreements. Lee was a "night-person" (as was Sharon) and she, Lorraine, was a "day-person." Why does one always have to marry the other? she laughed.

But it was no joke sometimes — when Lee and Sharon were late for school. Lorraine felt their tardiness was a terrible reflection upon *her*. She resented their attitude because she tried so hard; she couldn't understand why they — anyone — couldn't get out of bed in the morning. She didn't find it easy herself. But all you did was put both your feet on the floor and push — and *of course* you didn't want to, and *of course* your stomach heaved a little, and *of course* you thought the world could get along without you. You could always kill yourself, if it came to that. But in the meantime *you got up*.

She called first from the bottom of the stairs. "Lee," and then, "Sharon." When she did not hear them stir in the next few minutes, she went upstairs and gently shook each in

18

turn. She suspected that they were only pretending to be asleep and said so. "O come *on* — no games this morning, I haven't the patience." But they lay still in their beds until she was beside herself with vexation, begging them please to get up, they'd be late for school, they *had* to get up. They drove her to tears — and then they were irritated with her as if it were her fault.

"Why do you have to take it so seriously?"

It was unfair. She was right. The world said she was right. You were supposed to get up. She got up. And they made her feel wrong. It was unfair.

But Lee tried to explain to Lorraine that he and Sharon were night people; they liked staying up late — that's when you had *something to say*, for god's sake; they needed to sleep late in the morning. What was she so upset about? Lots of people slept late in the mornings, it was genetic. It sure as hell was not worth working yourself into a fit over, not worth *weeping*, for god's sake. Who cares, for god's sake? The school wasn't going to fall down if he wasn't there right on time. He wasn't going to get fired just because he was late sometimes. Lots of people were late; it was *expected*. But it was not worth making such a *goddamned* fuss about. *Stop crying*!

In fact it was a standing joke at the school that Mr. Branaman was often tardy and showed up looking puffy and obviously unshaven. He took the inevitable teasing with good humor.

Sharon was of course tardy as well, and her teachers resented the fact that she took her tardiness *as her right*, just because her father was a teacher. They couldn't punish her without getting him in hot water, of course, and none of them wanted to do that. They felt themselves put into an impossible situation, which made them resent both Lee and his daughter.

But they did try to separate the two in their minds. "Lee

Branaman was a disorganized person, but he laughed a lot. Sharon was almost . . . well, 'impertinent' is too sharp a word for it, and not many would say she was 'sullen' — she was too rosy for that, she had a marvelous complexion, but she was perhaps *withdrawn* — some would say obdurate. She stared at you as if you *simply didn't count*."

"Look," one teacher said, "if you got us all in a room and gave us cookies and hot chocolate, we'd all tell you what a good guy Lee Branaman was. We'd tell you that everybody liked him and he always had a cheerful hello when he came in the staff room. And that would be true, too.

"But if you got each of us alone — over a drink in the Poacher's Lounge, late at night, why, we might say that Lee 'had his problems.' The kids didn't like him. We're not supposed to know that, but of course we do. Word gets around. You hear it in the halls. One kid says he's got to go to Branaman's class and the other kid doesn't say anything in reply, doesn't even groan in sympathy. The silence is the judgment, eh? Worse than the groan. And it was a mistake to have his own daughter in his homeroom. The other kids resented that.

"He was tough on the kids, which they generally respect. You teach for a while and you know that sometimes a kid challenges you just because he needs the attention, he *wants* to get whacked back in line, put to work.

"But Lee Branaman wasn't *fair*. He and Sharon came strolling in ten minutes late in the morning and the bell rang before he'd finished taking roll — but he'd make the whole class sit there until he was done — and then they were late to the next class, which pissed off the next teacher, even if he or she knew who was responsible.

"There were stories, too, that he tangled with some of the tough kids pretty bad.

"Nothing ever came of it. A tough kid won't give you the

satisfaction of complaining about you. He'll take what you give out and be proud of it.

"Well, the last day he taught, Lee Branaman was supposed to have tangled pretty bad with a kid who was a known behavior problem. Guess who? Stringy Keeler, that's who. Now some of us wonder if someday they're not going to find what's left of Lee Branaman's skeleton out in the woods somewhere, a rack of bones rolled up under a tree."

7

Lee's car — a brand new Lincoln — disappeared with him. It was a flashy car, with a beige vinyl hardtop and a padded beige vinyl spare-tire hump in the trunk. Lorraine thought it was absurd, French, in poor taste. But she had long since given up arguing with Lee about cars. He wanted his own way about cars; and he wouldn't let her drive his car, said he'd get her one of her own — and he did — a nice little second-hand cinnamon-brown Volaré two-door. Her current car was Japanese. But he bought himself a big new car every other year. Why should she object to that? he said. They could afford it. His father always bought a new car every two years. You actually saved on your transportation costs that way, and if it involved tying up some of your assets in a new car — well, they had the money; that was one of the advantages of being the only son of a successful father. He might loathe his late father, but his father was certainly no fool, and buying a new car every other year was not *squandering* money but merely using assets economically — and if she didn't understand *that*, he wasn't going to waste time talking to her.

He went into the front room and curled himself into a fist in the corner chair and refused to say anything more.

He did that with his mother, too — and it shocked Lorraine because she knew how much he cared for his mother. He kissed his mother every morning when he came down for breakfast. Lorraine had never known anybody to do that. But Lorraine and Lee hadn't been in the house a week (and Lee's father hadn't been buried a month) before Lee was badgering his mother to buy them a new car. And she didn't refuse — she simply said "not yet" — but that wasn't the answer Lee wanted and he went into the front room to sulk.

His mother explained wryly to Lorraine that she had probably already discovered Lee could charm the birds out of the trees when he wanted to — but he didn't always want to. His mother referred to her only son as her "problem child."

But Mrs. Branaman had been good to Lorraine and seemed to accept her quite willingly — although Lorraine thought it was because she feared being presented with someone much worse as a daughter-in-law. Mrs. Branaman seemed surprised to find that Lorraine did *not* slop around the house smoking cigarettes, and instead tried to make herself useful. Lorraine resented that attitude a little

— on her own behalf as well as on Lee's. It was a terrible judgment on Lee, when you stopped to think about it.

But Lorraine soon realized that her mother-in-law was quite generous. She took Lorraine downtown shopping, and bought clothes for Lorraine without seeming to impose a taste on her — although of course she did, in effect. She took Lorraine to small shops where she knew the women owners by their first names, and she chatted with them about mutual interests while Lorraine tried on clothes. They assessed her choices shrewdly. *Good* meant that the dress should be purchased. *Suitable, nice, respectable*, and *stylish* did not necessarily mean unreserved approval. It was sometimes difficult to know. She was young, frightened, pregnant, overwhelmed. Lorraine did not dare go into Zeller's anymore, or even Sears. She felt guilty about all the clothes her mother-in-law was buying for her — in view of her thickening waist.

And Mrs. Branaman was herself not well. You could see the pain lines around her mouth — and the stiff walk concealing sharp bites of pain. Mrs. Branaman stopped short and peered into the window of a hardware store.

"Are you all right?" asked Lorraine.

"Yes. Of course," smiled Mrs. Branaman. You had to admire her lovely brown eyes — which Lee had not inherited. But she wasn't all right at all.

Lorraine admired her mother-in-law's courage, in the face of pain, and tried to emulate it — by vomiting as quietly as she could in the mornings, wanting to spare Mrs. Branaman the awkward information for as long as possible. But there was only the one bathroom in the large house, and silence wasn't easy. It was comic, really. She tried to hold back the noise while letting loose her stomach — and Lee said she sounded like a cat heaving. He said he had a great desire to bundle her out the door — only teasing, of course. But one morning, after kissing his mother, Lee announced that he

and Lorraine were expecting.

"I'm glad for you," his mother replied. "Quite sincerely."

But Mrs. Branaman died before Sharon was born, so Lee's mother never knew that Lee had gotten Lorraine pregnant well before the wedding. They were lucky in this respect, Lorraine guessed. She was ashamed to have Lee's mother know that Lee had persuaded her to go all the way — more than once, laughing and saying he loved her — and not to worry — he was rich. Ho-ho.

When she told Lee she was going to have a baby he sat down on the steps of the nurses' residence and wept. "How could you?" he said. "How could you?" He said he thought nurses knew how to take precautions.

"You said you didn't care."

He claimed he *never* said so and wept all the more. But he *had* said he didn't care — more than once.

He took his mother's death hard, and wept quite openly at her funeral. Lorraine was embarrassed for him and for his mother. His mother would have been embarrassed by this display. She was such a dignified woman.

But just as soon as he could after the funeral Lee went out and bought the car his mother had refused to buy for them.

8

The police spokesman said that the first thing they did after
the attempted robbery was check Gibby's Junkyard. Stringy
Keeler was a suspect from the beginning — from the
description, eh? At least, they *tried* to check Gibby's Junkyard. They went out there — and what they might have
seen in the distance was Stringy Keeler running away
through the miles of junk, disappearing into the bush
beyond, or they might have been seeing a cloud-shadow
skipping through the wrecked cars, or it might have been
Gibby himself. When Gibby decided to go on a three-day
drunk he got serious about it. He didn't want to be interrupted by anyone. He took his bottles and went into one of
the wrecked cars and drank and slept and shat there for
three days.

Why didn't the police go in?

The dogs.

Gibby has a whole god-damned *tribe* of dogs breeding
with one another out there and he doesn't make any
attempt to train them and damn little to feed them. He's
the only one they'll let in. So we was at the fence and all
we could see for sure was these dogs — this damned pack
of junkyard dogs — snuckered down in attack position —
and their eyes. Yellow eyes. You don't have to believe that
if you don't want to, but they had yellow eyes.

Then three days later Gibby shows up at the station, said
he heard we were looking for him, what the fuck for? We
said we were looking for his son Stringy. Who? he says. We
said we were looking for one Stringy Keeler.

Stringy was none of his concern, he said. He hadn't seen
Stringy in — what? Months, weeks? Stringy sometimes

came by after he got out of Kingston hoping for a motor-cycle to be brought in, but you know about motorcycle wrecks, says Gibby: there ain't much left over after.

God, that man *stank* — drink, dogs, grease, and human excrement.

But we went back out to the Junkyard with Gibby. We cleaned the police vehicle afterwards, let me assure you. We went inside the yard with Gibby, and the dogs kept circling us like wolves. He got a big kick out of that. We didn't think it was so very damned funny. They surrounded us and so there was always one or more at your back and you thought that if they attacked you might be able to shoot one but the rest of them would tear the flesh off your bones before you hit the ground.

You could see where Gibby did his drinking. He'd foul one old car and then another. He slept with the dogs and wasn't any more particular about his personal sanitation than they were.

So we asked him of course how Stringy got along with the dogs. He pretended not to know. We kind of persisted. "Jesus," he said, "you'll have to ask them — hee, hee, hee." Disgusting old bastard.

9

But within the week, one of the city detectives, off duty at the time, said he spotted Stringy down by the river near the Little League ball diamond. No mistake, he said, he knew Stringy. But when the uniformed police got there, there was no sign of him. They got out of the police car and walked down the gravel road, calling out. They felt silly. There was a haze coming in off the river — it had been a warm day, and the evening was cooling off. "Hey Stringy — c'mon — we want to talk to you."

The two policemen did not take the assignment seriously. They didn't really expect him to answer; they were just going through the motions. They talked gossip about the off-duty detective who had spotted Stringy, wondering, ho-ho, just where he was off to when he spotted Stringy. The uniformed policemen briefly considered plunging into the undergrowth alongside the river to look for him, but decided there was no point to it — they'd make so much noise he'd be gone before they could catch him, slipping through the underbrush like a snake.

"Hey Stringy, c'mon — we want to talk to you." Shit. Not a hope.

They got back into the police car and when the doors slammed shut and the motor started, Stringy breathed easier. He hadn't been far away — he could hear them gossiping like a couple of fucking old ladies about the off-duty detective. He didn't dare raise his head because he thought sure they'd notice him. He kept his nose down in the damp earth, eyes closed. God, that was hard! You expected any moment to get shot in the back, executed, cop guys playing justice. Jesus!

He was shaking — soaking wet. He'd spent the day in his shelter, really just a piece of plastic, and had sweated like a bastard. Now they were gone, the silly shits, he thought they would never catch him — unless they offered him a Big Mac. He'd kill for a Big Mac right now. Shit. Everything had gone wrong as it usually did, shit, you were nothing but a doomed animal, marked for justice, as they say. Shit. He hugged himself tight, wrapped his tattooed arm around his neck. Shit, shit, shit. Shit, shit, shit. He tried to clench himself into sleep, and, after a while, when he had given up trying, succeeded.

When he woke up it was dark and fucking *cold*. He was shaking. He crawled out of his shelter, shaking all over, cursing — not at the cold but at the shaking. Wouldn't it ever fucking stop? He ran around in little circles feeling silly. Fuck O Fuck! This was no way to treat a man. He took off on a beeline for Sharon's house. What he was going to do was sit on her porch on the swing the way he used to do when they were in Grade Seven together. What he used to do, the next day in the schoolyard, was say to her, "Hey — you better iron them clothes like your mother wants — she's some pissed off with you."

"Are you listening outside my house?"

He laughed and tapped his head. "I *know*," he said. "I *know*."

"You stop doing that!" she said, meaning the listening. She stamped her foot. Looked silly as hell, there on the playground. But he was just paying her back for being so snooty on the playground during school hours — at night in the same place it was a different story. She gave him hand-jobs right where they were standing, pumped him out on the ground. "You like that?" she asked sweetly. But she wouldn't give him anything more, there was no sense asking or trying. It was a hand-job or nothing and one night she just walked away leaving him stiff because she was pissed off with him. Fuck! He couldn't even run after her. He felt ridiculous, felt like killing her, which she fucking deserved. So what he did without exactly intending to was tell that suck Billy M. she was putting out. Billy M. of course told everybody and old Branaman must of heard because the next day he was standing by Stringy's desk with a piece of paper in his hand shouting, "What do you call this? What do you call this, eh?" Stringy didn't know what the fuck he was talking about. It was one of Stringy's arithmetic papers. Stringy was failing arithmetic. He was failing everything, ask him if he gave a fuck. But he didn't know what the fuck was going on, and then Branaman was slashing at him with one of those metal-edged rulers and Jesus! it hurt! Blood was running down his face and he was out of the classroom and down the hall crying out "you fucker! you fucker!" and thinking Branaman was going to pay, he was going to fucking pay.

Sharon had to sit there and endure it, continue to endure it when her father told the class to "Shut Up, Shut Up!" And nobody had said a word. He was shouting into silence; you could hear Stringy running crying down the hall. The entire class was on Stringy's side and they'd make life miserable for her. Why hadn't her father thought of that? *She* could get beaten up, didn't he know that? He was so naive in so many ways. He had the notion that boys wouldn't beat up girls. You'd think he'd grown up on another planet. He believed what he wanted to believe. And it was a terrible mistake even to have mentioned Stringy's name to him. She wouldn't have, if she'd known he was going to react like this. She was just teasing him, that's all, telling him that *of course* the guys were after her, she was growing up, wasn't she, she was attractive, wasn't she? She was, she knew she was. She told her father that even Stringy was sweet on her. When her father didn't respond, she added that Stringy had put his hand on her bum — that's all. Just a little feel on the playground. Nothing much. Nothing unusual, Daddy.

Her father asked her if she encouraged him.

No, she said.

Her father said that there *were* girls who played with the boys in the bushes.

She gave her father a disgusted look. "I don't play," she said. He knew that.

And then he went and lost his temper in the classroom, and she was the one who was going to have to face the consequences.

Her father ran out of the classroom after Stringy and the

terrible silence continued. You could feel everyone considering. It was terrible. They were going to get her, she knew they were. They were going to get her.

II

Lorraine was heartsick when she heard of the incident. "Why can't you learn to control yourself?" she asked her husband.

Lee shrugged and told her not to work herself into a fit and, for god's sake, to stop weeping. She drove him up the wall when she started weeping.

Had he talked to Ginger?

Yes, he'd spoken to Ginger. Ginger called him in.

And?

"And he told me to 'sit down and talk' — how's that?"

Lorraine was determined to control herself.

"He asked me to explain. So I did."

"What did you tell him?"

"For Christ's sake, I told him just what I've told you. That the kid was a known behavior problem and if he didn't believe me he could read the kid's file, that the kid told me to *fuck off* and I told him I wouldn't tolerate language like that in my classroom, and he took a swing at me. Jesus — if we let kids get away with that kind of stuff, the next step's Anarchy. Even you should see that! Now god-damn it stop crying. All I did was defend myself, I didn't realize I had the ruler in my hand."

"Will there be charges?" Lorraine asked.

"From that little shit? No there won't be any charges from young Mr. Keeler, believe you me. He might burn the house down, but there won't be any charges . . . O god-damn it, don't look so fucking *stricken*. I'll sit up and keep watch — you don't have to worry, go to bed."

Lorraine told him there was no point in telling somebody not to worry after something like this. People worried. Did he expect her to sleep after something like this, after he told her the boy might burn down the house?

Of course she couldn't go to sleep. She lay in bed full of fear. And she knew Lee well enough to know that it might just be a story he made up to torment her. It wouldn't take much to burn down this old house, the wood was dried out. It was all too easy to imagine the roar of the flames around her and no escape. He mocked her because she imagined too many horrible things, and she did, she wouldn't deny that. From the second floor there would be no escape and then Lee and his darling daughter could live alone in peace. The central stairway would be an inferno, she would never be able to make her way outside.

She heard Lee and Sharon talking in the study but, as usual, she couldn't make out what was being said. It must have been difficult for Sharon to watch — a boy in her class fighting with her father.

After a while Lorraine dozed into awkward dreams and

when she heard Sharon come upstairs and go to bed, she fell into an uneasy sleep. She awoke in terror.

She didn't know from what. She leapt out of bed and ran to the head of the staircase. She thought that she should have put on a robe, what if there were a fire? But she was barefoot. She did not smell any smoke, didn't hear anything, but something was wrong.

She made her way downstairs and looked for Lee in the study, but he wasn't there. He wasn't in the kitchen, either, or the front room. She was afraid to go down to the basement. She checked the front door. It was firmly closed and locked, but the chain wasn't on. He'd gone out, then. She went out to see if he was sitting on the porch-swing in the dark, but he wasn't. It was cold and she felt vulnerable. She shivered.

She returned to the kitchen. She sat in the kitchen until it began to turn light.

Then she got dressed and went out to look for Lee. She walked over to the school, which was only three blocks away. The sun was not yet up; the light was a thin grey. There was a light on in the hallway of the school and Lorraine went to the front doors and yanked on them. The doors were chained shut as well as locked to prevent vandalism, and Lorraine made a terrible demented noise which echoed through the empty school. She frightened herself by what she was doing.

She returned home and sat in the kitchen until it was time to call Sharon to go to school. Sharon came down in her own good time, as usual, and her mother's mouth was full of bitterness from lack of sleep and worry. She told Sharon that her father would not be going to school today, so Sharon went off by herself.

12

Anyway, she would not be visiting her father's study again, that was one thing sure, even if he begged her. He said he never begged her, and she said he was right, she supposed, not in so many words, but he looked so utterly hurt that she felt sorry for him. They had spats about it. "Don't visit if you don't want to," he said; and she replied, "I won't." But last night she had gone to see him because she was very angry, *rightly* angry. The other kids would *get* her, didn't he know?

Yes, he said, he knew, he was sorry, sorry *only* about that.

Would he get fired?

No, he wouldn't get fired. If it had been anybody but Stringy Keeler, he might have been in trouble, but not with young Mr. Keeler. *Why*, he said, *why* did she let Stringy fondle her bum?

She did not *let* Stringy fondle her bum, she pointed out. He came up behind and grabbed her.

Why didn't she slap him?

"O Daddy, you don't understand *any*thing sometimes!"

He nodded. That was true. He opened his arms to her and she came to sit on his lap as she usually did and he put his face to her neck and kissed her just under her ear where, as she used to say, it tickled nice. She snuggled herself against him and let herself go. You closed your eyes and let yourself go and everything was warm and comforting. The glow from the lamp was a golden ball in her dreaming; the smell of her father was dear. She murmured that it was sweet and warm and he murmured the words in return to her.

"I love you," she said.

"I love you," he said, and she let herself go loose as a sleeping rag doll and let things happen, it was all right, until suddenly he flung her off, oh she was angry! She knew exactly what had happened. This time he had his thing out, and she was furious, why couldn't he control himself, why couldn't he be nice to her, it wasn't *fair*, it wasn't *fair*, she ran upstairs furious with him!

What if her mother heard them? She thought her mother was just looking for an *excuse* to go crazy. Her mother wanted to drown herself in self-pity, her mother wanted to babble herself into a nervous breakdown to spite them both, to show them both, to say, "Now see what you've done?"

Hysterics, her father said, was the way weak people controlled others.

In the morning her mother could barely get out the words. "Your father won't be going to school today," and a wave of dread swept through Sharon, wondering what in the world he might have said to her mother, and now she was going to have to face everything at school alone. It wasn't fair.

And in fact her punishment was not long in coming. The other kids took Lee Branaman's absence as understandable. Sharon kept her head down, pretending to study. She thought the others were children. No one came to take roll and no one closed the door to the classroom. Old Ginger came roaming by after announcements on the loud-speaker and said, "No teacher yet?"

Sharon did not look up. Old Ginger did not dare ask her where her father was. The rules of decorum were much too strict for that. He went back to his office to telephone around for a supply-teacher. There was no point telephoning Branaman's house — Mrs. Branaman worked at the hospital. And what if Branaman himself answered? It would be far too awkward.

The kids had long since decided that Branaman was staying home because he was afraid of Stringy. It was a bit fantastic, okay, but they knew that Stringy was a mean little fucker and they wouldn't put it past him to bring a knife to school and probably Branaman feared so as well. So of course he stayed home. He wasn't a complete idiot.

But Stringy didn't show up either. At least she didn't have to face him.

The girls had their revenge on Sharon that afternoon. It was after gym class, in the dressing room. While Sharon was still in the shower some of the girls took her clothes and stuffed them in a toilet. Then someone peed on them.

Sharon walked home wearing her gym clothes under her coat.

She did not tell her mother what had happened. She did not want any sympathy from her mother, any understanding. She was angry with her mother because none of this would have happened, she thought, if only her mother had been a better wife to her father.

13

There were any number of ways he could have killed himself with the car. He could have attached a hose from the exhaust pipe and run it through a window — parked the car out on a logging road in the woodlot the other side of the Trans-Canada. A black ribbed hose exactly the right size was available from Canadian Tire. You were supposed to attach it to a sump pump.

Or, his life in ruin (totally fucked up career and everything else), he could tear out the Trans-Canada and aim the car off the road just above the dam. Recently they'd pulled some cars out of there — some sort of stolen car insurance scam. This time one of them could have a body in it.

The police pooh-poohed the idea that Stringy Keeler might have murdered Lee Branaman. Stringy might be a "mean little fucker" in schoolyard terms, and he might well have carried a knife to school — you'd be surprised how many boys do. But they usually carry it just for the show of power it gives them — the walk, the swagger of somebody with a secret. But, look, Stringy was only thirteen at the time of the incident, and not big for his age. He was about the average height for a thirteen-year-old boy — and that meant that he was almost a foot shorter and forty pounds lighter than Lee Branaman. It was pretty difficult to imagine him lugging Lee's dead body into the woods to a secluded grave.

Moreover, Stringy made no attempt to run away. He did not return to school, but he did not leave town, either. He was seen hanging around the Mall near the high school, just another of the scraggy mall-rats who drift in and out of the arcade, sit on the benches with their buddies smoking and laughing suddenly at nothing very much at all. From time to time the security staff suggested that maybe he ought to go elsewhere. He seemed quick to agree and left — only to slip right back into the Mall by another entrance. The Security Guard they called Old Fart right to his face said, "You want me to call the Police? I will."

"Big fucking deal," said Stringy.

"If you end up in court you can get banned from the Mall."

"Fuck you," said Stringy.

The educational authorities telephoned Gibby, who said he had no idea where the kid was and why didn't they go fuck themselves. When you were met with belligerence like that there was nothing you could do, really. Oh yeah, you *could* call the police, but at best they'd just go through the motions. They had better things to do than chase after some guy who denied he was the kid's father anyway. What you have are legal options which are theoretical but impractical. If somebody doesn't *want* to comply with the law, he doesn't. You have to *agree* to the law before it can be enforced. That's true, that's the way it is, really.

You know what the problem is? At sixteen these kids can go to Welfare and tell Welfare they can't get along with their parents or whatever and Welfare will rent them an apartment. Jesus! That's true. Three of them get together and god knows what they do — mountain bikes and skateboards, dress themselves up like rock stars from outer space, get their ghetto-blasters, and then go out and make *din* at 2 a.m. They like making noise for the sake of making noise, eh? Noise is *Good*. It pisses people off. That's *Good*. So they get drunk and zip around on their skateboards at two in the morning, and what burns your ass is that they're still children! They're out there in the middle of the night playing. They're children!

Stringy was charged with drinking under age and possession of liquor in an unauthorized place (the Mall) and, eventually, with creating a disturbance. He assaulted a police constable with his fists, drunk. He was taller now, but still scrawny. He never would fill out much. He had a short stay in the Training School. He passed out in front of Shoppers Drug Mart. He pissed on a car in the parking lot — a police car.

"Most of these kids," said one of the staff at the Training School, "have a completely unrealistic view of themselves. They have an unattainable dream of themselves, and then they blame everybody *but* themselves for their failure to attain the dream. I blame TV.

"For example, I said to Stringy, what do you want to be. You're not entirely stupid, I said. What do you want to be? What kind of a job do you want?

" 'I want to be a rock star,' he says.

"I told him that it was the twelfth time today that I'd heard the same crazy wish.

"He said he wanted to be on TV: bang-bang-bang.

"Uh-huh, I said. What can you do?

" 'I can do anything, man,' he said. 'Anything.'

"Get real, I said. He couldn't do shit. Bluntly. No sense talking fancy to these kids. What kind of trade you want, I said. Small engine repair?

" 'I want to drive a bulldozer,' he said. Heavy equipment. And he figured — he figured that if he could just get to *Alberta* he could get a job driving a bulldozer. Just like that! He figured that when he was eighteen it would just happen — if he could get to *Alberta*. Doesn't that burn your ass? What he wanted to do was play with *toys*. He wanted big *toys*.

"Then what? I said.

"Then, he said, he was going to get himself a big black fucking motorcycle. 'A Harley,' he said, 'not one of those jap junk jobs.' "

14

What he did was walk up to her in the Tim Horton Donut Shop and say, "Hi, how you doin'?" She looked like she was going to fucking faint.

But that wasn't true — the fainting part. She had seen him come in and half-expected him to speak to her, but he was half-drunk at the time, was it any wonder that she put him down with a polite smile and returned to her coffee cup? She felt herself that she had just passed a heart-pounding test — Stringy was a test; she'd known that for some time, not that she believed for a moment that he had murdered her father. But you couldn't help seeing him around town (up at the Mall, for example, hanging around Dooby's late at night by the hot dog stand), and every time she saw him she was reminded of her father's arm slashing down with the metal-edged ruler and the fine spray of blood fanning out from Stringy's head and then her father gone, disappeared. So she prepared herself constantly for the sight of Stringy, looked for him everywhere all the time. No scar. You could not help but think of murder, though. You could not help but think of your missing father dead.

There were other tests as well. Everytime some new kid joined the class as they went up through the grades, the *story* was whispered to him or her (unless the person was a complete nerd — because the *story* was kind of a welcoming gift you gave to a kid everybody agreed to accept), and then Sharon would catch glances directed at her reflected in the windows beside the classroom, people staring at her because of the *story*. They kept her out of things because of the *story*.

Other tests just made her sardonic. Guys making reference to her figure in the hallways of the high school. They didn't have the nerve to ask her out because of the *story*. She was considered stuck-up and different. But that didn't stop them from making comments about her. The guys standing outside Grimson's door snickered when they looked at her and remarked, "Nice tits." She passed those tests by ignoring them. They didn't bother her in the least.

Nice tits.

But home life wasn't exactly great, either. She and her mother did not get along. Her mother accused her of sneaking up to the Mall to meet boys, and what could be more ridiculous? She did not *sneak*, said Sharon. She was furious. She blamed her mother for everything. Did her mother want her to bring somebody home here? Could her mother possibly imagine kids coming *here* to drink cokes and eat munchies? It was ridiculous. Her mother replied that she didn't see anything wrong with this house, so Sharon, in a rage, picked out a boy in computer class, a jock who was expected to be drafted by the NHL but who couldn't handle a keyboard if his life depended upon it, and brought him home in his athletic jacket to meet her mother, without warning her.

It was as if she had brought home a prize for which she had nothing but contempt. It was a very awkward time; the poor guy didn't know what to do, and her mother was furious with Sharon for embarrassing the boy. He was not a classy guy; he came from out the roads somewhere and rode the schoolbus; he had no talent in the world except for sports. He was nothing.

Her mother accused Sharon of mocking her and making fun of poor people, and Sharon said some people deserved to be mocked, and her mother slapped her.

Sharon was stunned. No one had ever dared slap her before, and, she realized, she was never going to allow anyone to slap her again.

"If you ever do that again," said Sharon, "I'll kill you."

15

Then, on the day after Christmas, the 30th, the deadest day of a dead year, her father telephoned her. He knew her mother would be at work.

Daddy, Daddy, Daddy! The world turned upside down.

O Daddy, Daddy, Daddy. She was weeping while he was trying to explain — he had to explain, he said — he was trying to explain that he had tried to turn the wheels of the car hard right, but he couldn't do it. She didn't understand, continued to cry. What — two years?

No, she had the exact number: two years and eight months.

She had not expected this, was not prepared for this, she thought he was dead, and he said that when he got to that place on the Trans-Canada, just above the dam, eh? —

where he had to turn right, he couldn't do it, he just couldn't do it, he was thinking of her.

She wept. He had cursed himself for a coward, he said. He was saying what he had planned to say. He said he had planned to kill himself but it didn't work.

O Daddy, Daddy, Daddy.

He'd stolen some bread in Quebec and thought he'd get caught, expected the sirens and the flashing lights of the Quebec police, but nobody bothered and he had to keep going.

O Daddy, Daddy, Daddy.

Then he'd got to Toronto and got a motel room and expected not to be able to pay for it and be arrested but then he stumbled on a job and so everything was all right, he wanted to send her a Christmas present but couldn't. Now he had an idea.

O Daddy, Daddy, Daddy. We didn't *do* anything.

I know honey, we didn't. He couldn't afford to talk much longer, he said. He wasn't exactly rich these days. It was marvelous to hear her voice. Don't tell her mother.

O Daddy! She wouldn't! How could he think that!

Well, he had to say it, he said. She understood, didn't she? And he told her how to get a post office box so he could send her things like a Christmas present, maybe some money now and then. He had a job selling shoes. It didn't pay much, but he had his head above water, he said. He missed her, he said.

O she missed him, too!

He had to hang up now, he had to go. Still love me?

O yes! she said.

When she hung up she had to run out of the house because the house was too small to contain her joy, she was overjoyed, thank God her mother wouldn't be home for another four hours. She wanted to skip like a child. What she'd have to do this evening was go to the Mall or a movie or something so she didn't give herself and her father away with happiness.

In the Mall she kept an eye out for Stringy, as usual. She saw him; he was just being escorted out of the Mall by a Security Guard. She'd won, she thought; she'd won after all.

16

He was drinking a lot of beer these days, what the fuck, whose business was it anyway? What was next was another beer, and what came after that was another beer. Get fuzzed. He was living in a shit place with Match and Tracy. Only shit places would rent to Welfare. You can imagine the landlord. Tracy was nineteen and a bit retarded but she would fuck anytime and could buy beer for the three of them, no hassle. There were empties lined up on the window-sill, Trace would take them to the bottle-dealer when she came back. It was time to blow this fucking town.

Trace was always available, but no fun, she'd just do what you told her, it was like fucking a donut. Hah! Like fucking a donut. Another beer.

For a while he and Match stole mountain bikes and wrecked them or threw them over the bridge into the river. Then they almost got caught because Match was so fucking slow. Fuck, Stringy could run twice as fast drunk as Match could sober. Then Trace got picked up shoplifting Zeller's and Match ran away leaving Stringy to deal with the fucking landlord. Stringy drank half of his last beer and poured the other half over the TV set making it fizz and crackle and go puff. Best thing on it, he thought, he was moving towards the door, already going west. He'd go to Calgary the White City where he saw his hands on some pretty fucking important machinery. He was tough. Tough guy. Mean little fucker. They'd be surprised at what he could do. He saw his hands handling oily chain, dangerous job in the fucking oil fields like in the beer commercials. Shit, he could do a job like that if the fuckers would give him a chance.

He told a trucker in the Bypass Restaurant he'd help him unload if he gave him a ride to Calgary. The trucker ignored him and when Stringy repeated the offer the trucker told Stringy he expected a whole lot for god-damned little, didn't he? Did he have any idea how far it was to Calgary? Stringy said he didn't give a fuck. The driver said he'd give Stringy a ride west a ways, but he didn't want any mouthing off, that understood? Stringy shrugged and the driver said he'd take that as agreement, and they rolled off, Stringy freezing in the fucking cab and asking the driver why he didn't turn on the fucking heat and the driver said he was comfortable, you got too much heat in a cab it made you sleepy, sleepy got you killed. He talked about rolling rigs — rigs he'd seen rolled, stories he'd heard, people killed, all the way to Montreal. Stringy was fucking starving and had to piss. They didn't stop in Montreal. It was dark and they didn't go into the city, you could just see it on the other side of the river twinkling, French. The driver read the highway signs and told Stringy what they meant. "You have to know that here," he said, "you want to truck through the damn place." He was god-damn proud of himself. Stringy said "shit" and the driver asked him if he wanted to get out right here?

Stringy didn't say anything more for a long time. They were into Ontario and the sign said Service Centre and Stringy could see the bright lights and he said he had to piss but the driver ignored him. He was enjoying Stringy's discomfort, the bastard. Stringy was squirming and having a really hard time being quiet and the bastard driver really enjoyed that and they were down the road a long way before Stringy said if the driver didn't stop he was going to piss on the floor of the god-damned cab and the driver said that if Stringy knew what was good for him he'd piss in his pants first and Stringy got his cock out, said he couldn't hold it and the driver laughing like a bastard slowed the rig down and stopped beside the road and Stringy hopped down squirting, was standing there pissing in full stream when the bastard driver pulled away leaving Stringy screaming cocksucker at him. Gone. Left. You could see the lights of a little town over there a ways. He headed there, screaming cocksucker at the departed trucker.

Cocksucker. He had to walk maybe three miles full of rage at the trucker before he came to the first lights of the fucking little motel. He thought about holding up the fucking place, but didn't. He asked for a room instead, he had some welfare cash left over, he didn't give a shit if it was all gone tomorrow, he wanted to get some sleep. He asked the woman clerk for a room with hot and cold running blondes and she gave him a stare which was supposed to make him feel like a little turd. Fucking bitch better watch out. The room was panelled with varnished plywood like in Grade Seven shop class and cut-out ducks flew up a wall. He didn't know what time it was when he woke up, hungrier than a bastard, thinking about a few beers. He made his way out into the dark of the town, must have been 3 a.m. or something like that, nothing moving but a cop car. He stepped around a corner of a building when he saw the cop car nosing down the street. Fuckers. They'd grab him if they had the chance, ask him what the fuck he was doing there. They passed by. He was cold. He looked for a McDonald's, didn't see one, or someplace to buy beer, didn't see anything — and felt terribly alone. God-damned place didn't even have a mall. He saw himself explaining his plight to Match. He felt cut adrift, frightened. He could have been drifting into a black space in an arcade game for all he knew, shit, he was shivering. He went back to the motel, hungry, there had to be someplace he could get something to eat, Jesus, he crawled into bed, shivering, even when he was warm he was shivering, he felt like he was leaving himself, having an attack of some sort, shit. He fell into a horrible sleep and woke up to daylight and drool all over his pillow. What he wanted was a beer, something to eat, he was fucking starving. Did they expect him to starve to death? He got himself out the door, it was afternoon, the lady who had rented him the room was bent over a flowerbed, her fat ass up in the air, the sunlight was fucking blinding. The street was no better but he found a restaurant where he ordered a hamburger and beer and the guy at the counter told him they didn't serve beer and Stringy thought the guy meant he wasn't going to serve him, Stringy, and so he told the guy he had money, but the guy just looked at Stringy as if he thought Stringy was a Retard or something which really pissed Stringy off and said they didn't have a license. Stringy thought he'd like to open the guy up like a can, just show everybody the guy's

47

rotten guts. The hamburger was covered with cooked onions, all stringy. Stringy said to the guy, "This hamburger tastes like shit," and the guy told Stringy he could get out right now. "Fuck you," said Stringy, leaving. Didn't pay for the fucking hamburger, neither, he thought he'd tell Match, swaggering. I'm a mean fucker. "Don't come back," the guy said. Stringy walked back to the fucking motel needing a beer bad, fuck, he was almost out of money and he didn't even know where the fuck he was. He would tell Match: I didn't even know where the fuck I was, somewhere in Ontario, that's all I knew then. But I knew I was being jerked around, you know? The room seemed so god-damned small. What he needed was a beer, the lady wasn't working in the flowers anymore, she was back in the end room with the neon "Office" sign turned off now. His stomach didn't feel good; that god-damned slimy hamburger. He lay on his bed shivering like a bastard, thinking he'd say to Match never eat a hamburger in wherever-the-fuck this was. He got up and tried to throw up in the toilet but couldn't. He was sick, shit. His head was fucking pounding. He turned on the TV set and the reception was fucking terrible, there was this girl's head bouncing up and down and she's going yah-yah-yah and then she speeded up zip, zip, zip, shit. He kicked the set but that didn't do any good. He lay down on the bed and pulled his knees up to his chest, moaning, what he needed was a beer or two to run the shit through his body and fart away the pain, his head pounding, it was late, hell, evening, his head was still pounding, he didn't feel any better, it had started raining. Raining. Shit.

He counted his money. He didn't have enough to stay another night. It was raining.

He got out his pocket knife, head pounding, and went out to rob the motel.

Which wouldn't have been so bad — not good, but not

quite so bad — if he hadn't cut the flower bed woman and she screamed like a bastard and when the police caught up with him by the town library he didn't know what the fuck was going on and threw down his jack-knife, saying "I'm sick, I'm sick, I'm sick," not that they gave a fuck because they threw him into the cruiser and he caught a knee in the face and blood was coming out of his nose down his face when they hustled him into the police station, his nose was gushing, he liked that, felt good, looked good, he thought.

When he got into the cop station he threw up all over the floor and that didn't help one god-damned bit either.

17

(Mrs.) Amy Barlow said at the trial that she did not think Keeler intended to hurt her — exactly. What he seemed — mostly — was confused and angry. That wasn't to say she wasn't frightened of him. She had been frightened of him when he checked in the night before. She thought he might be an escapee or somebody on the run. They were so handy to the U.S. border, you know. And he did look angry — but he also looked so young that she found it difficult to take him seriously. She now realized that he was two months past his eighteenth birthday at the time of the assault, but when he walked in — that was surprising in itself, she said — people don't usually *walk* into a motel — she thought first of all how *young* he looked. But she was suspicious from the very beginning — but you can't *do* anything, can you, until they do something? She has two sons, she said, and he looked like one of the kids they used to bring home to supper — underfed. She wanted to feed him, she said — not Keeler, the boy her sons brought home. She did not like the look in Keeler's eye, she thought he looked angry and she decided he was best left to himself. He paid cash in advance — volunteered to do that. So, no — of course he did not seem to her like someone who was trying to beat the motel bill.

The prosecution suggested (when the opportunity arose) that he might well have been more than willing to pay in advance since he intended to steal it all back later anyway.

But she could not believe what was happening to her when he came in and showed her the knife. It was in the evening, after supper, it had started to rain, a cold rain.

"What did he say?"

She couldn't remember. She laughed nervously. "I was *so scared*," she said. He showed her the knife, and that was communication enough.

(Counsel for the defense suggested that inasmuch as he made no verbal demands he did not intend to rob the motel. It was pointed out further that because he used the *short* blade of the pocket-knife, a legal knife, he intended only to frighten her.)

"Did *you* say anything?"

"I can't remember. I was scared."

"Why did he slash at you?"

"I don't know. Maybe I wasn't moving fast enough for him, I don't know."

"But he did slash at you?"

"Like he was slapping me — I don't know. When he came in he was dancing around like a little boy who has to go to the bathroom, and he seemed angry and irritated, like he wanted to throw a tantrum and was just looking for an excuse."

"So he didn't intend to hurt you?"

"O yes he did! He slapped at me with the knife and it *stung*, it really *stung*, and I felt the blood . . ."

"Then he put his hand in the cashbox?"

"Yes. I felt the blood and I thought I'm going to be marked for life and I started to scream and he ran out and left the door open and the rain was coming in, I telephoned Larry down at the police station because I know him and he radioed the police car and they caught him running down the street."

No stitches were required to heal the cut; there was no permanent scar.

But it was the knife that got him the term at Kingston. He had carried it in a little leather holster. It was legal, but that didn't help, either.

18

Things get fastened onto you. There's nothing you can do about that. When Stringy was being interrogated at the police station (they led him away from his vomit on the floor, a cop cursing him), they asked him what he was doing there and he said he was on his way to Calgary. Jesus! Did these fuckers think he came all this way just to rob their fucking little motel? "I was going to Calgary to look for work."

"What kind of work do you do?"

Did they care? "I drive a bulldozer," he said.

One cop shook his head. "This sure as hell ain't the short route to Calgary," he said. "Do you have any idea where you are?"

Stringy's pause was a dead giveaway. "I don't give a fuck," he said.

"You don't even know where the hell you are, do you?"

Stringy tried to remember the name of the town on the cop car, and couldn't. It was then he realized he was in deep shit.

"I don't give a fuck," he said.

The cops started laughing, shaking their heads. What they meant by this gesture was that they thought Stringy was the *dumbest* little shit they had ever come across. Jesus, if he hadn't used the knife he might have walked away with probation — just because he was so stupid.

Years later, when the call came from the East enquiring about Stringy Keeler's previous arrest, the story changed just a little. The policeman who took the call said sure he remembered Stringy Keeler. He was the kid who thought that Lester, Ontario, was Calgary. You couldn't forget somebody that dumb, could you? They figured he was retarded.

19

The pre-sentencing report indicated that his educational skills were marginal. He could read at the Grade Five level, but his writing skills were barely those expected of a Grade Three pupil in Ontario schools. But — hey — that wasn't too bad, you know — most of these guys in prison can't read or write at all. You'd be surprised at how many of them *can't even tell time*! What their problem is — they can't understand that when they want something they can't just go take it. Oh, they figure out that somebody's not going to *let* them walk into a store and walk out with a new color TV. That's what we call *reason*. They can calculate that because someone somewhere along the line slapped their hands when they tried it. But they don't see anything *wrong* with slipping into the store at night and taking the damn thing. Look — that's the only way any of them have ever gotten anything at all! They can think *don't* but they can't think *wrong*. *Wrong* is fucking *abstract*; *steal* has a TV set attached to it. They think crime is necessary.

Was it for Stringy? Probably — although he thought he robbed the fucking motel because he was too fucking sick to think straight. Wasn't that the shits? Not stoned, not even drunk, but fucking *sick*. He blamed the hamburger.

So what he had when he was brought into the Pen was a label — armed robbery with violence. The word about Stringy was there before he was, not that it meant much. Stringy came in as an outsider, a man without a franchise. He was neither Indian nor French nor Biker. He was a wiry little shit among guys who did weights. He was lucky in his cell-mate (Willie Jay) and unlucky in Gagnon.

Gagnon was a big fucker (bald, forty) who had killed his common-law wife while he was stoned, and the fact was he didn't seem to have a brain left at all. He was a goof. Once he took his dink out in the dining hall and tried to piss in his mashed potatoes! That brought the guards running — and gained him no understanding at all! The incident was considered disgusting. Another crazy. But he did weights and he was a big fucker, so how was Stringy to know what to do when Gagnon jostled him in the line? Stringy thought it was a come-on of some sort and so he told Gagnon to keep his fucking hands to himself. Gagnon stared at him, uncomprehending, then said, "I own your ass."

Naturally — this was funny — Stringy figured (from what he'd heard) that Gagnon was going to fuck him up the ass, and he was terrified. He tried not to sleep (unsuccessfully) and kept his back to the wall. His cell-mate Willie Jay from Calgary (a joke there, Willie Jay said it was a shit place full of Indians) thought this was funny as hell. "How do you expect him to get in here?"

"Shit I don't know," said Stringy.

"Well the guy you got to fear most," said Willie Jay, "is me." But he was joking. Willie Jay was a good guy.

But he couldn't help Stringy when Gagnon caught Stringy in a corridor one day when Stringy was on his way to work in the kitchen, a real shit job. Gagnon really went at him — Christ, there were bruises all *over* his body and his nose was smashed and it looked like a gang beating for sure. Stringy of course said nothing, but everybody, including the prison administration, knew that it was Gagnon, but Gagnon was considered crazy so what the hell could you do? There was more blame attached to the god-damned guard who should have kept it from happening than there was to Gagnon. Gagnon was punished, but it didn't mean fuck to him. Time meant nothing to him. Everything was the present. Life meant nothing to him. It was just grunt, hit, scream.

But Stringy and Willie Jay were like a pair of rats, like a pair of rat-brothers. Stringy felt almost happy sometimes — and Jesus, the feeling was so strange he didn't almost fucking realize it. He and Willie Jay were jacking off at the same time one night talking about various girls, tits, cunts they'd known — trading the girls back and forth, laughing like hell — and it got better and better when the guys in the next cell got pissed off at them (pair of queers), which made them feel all the better when they came. 'Course, afterwards they felt a bit shitty and embarrassed and the swearing from the next cell continued until the guard came and that could mean really deep shit, but nothing happened. He and Willie Jay were a real pair. Willie Jay confessed he thought he was part Indian, guys were always asking him and he said he wasn't, he didn't think he was, but Jesus, you never knew, his mother was pretty careless he said, he laughed.

Willie Jay had a little tattooed bird on his arm, and when he jacked off he said he was making the bird shit. That was funny. He and Stringy talked tattoos. Stringy wanted a tattoo.

Things went wrong.

20

Willie Jay was paroled.

That was terrible.

Stringy felt naked.

They'd kind of looked after each other and without Willie Jay Stringy was always looking over his shoulder. He had to try to stay with other people so Gagnon couldn't get to him, but the god-damned other people were a risk, too. You had to watch who you talked to. You got a wrong label you were in deep shit.

"Hey — little fucker — get lost."

But that wasn't bad. Grin and move — but shit, he really

56

missed Willie Jay. Stringy thought that if he had Willie Jay's address he could send him a letter or something but he didn't have it. Shit. He was stuck in here and out there things were so fucking *huge*.

Scary things. A prison is never quiet — *never* — unless something bad is going to happen. When Stringy felt silence following him his skin crawled. Like he was in a bubble of silence when he went to the dining hall, nobody wanted to talk to him. He was so fucking scared he wanted to piss his pants, you didn't know what those guys could do to you. What they were doing now — he heard this at the table, they wanted him to hear this, they pointed it at him — was taking this guy who had AIDS and he fucked you up the ass, and that was it, you were walking death. He'd seen the guy. He looked like DEATH. What they did was bring him around and hold you against the wall and take your pants down and he did it to you. Stringy swore he could hear guys screaming in the night and there was one new guy who cried all the time and wouldn't talk to anyone, they were trying to get him transferred out of here.

Every so often you had to go see the psychologist and she talked at you for a while and asked you how your life was. She wasn't too bad-looking and why she was there, they figured, was because she liked the idea of what the cons wanted to do to her if they got half a chance, and she was just waiting for an incident where she could be the hostage, you'd better believe it. Take off her glasses and go at her. She'd never know who it was and she'd love it. But her office was just one little room in a batch of little offices in this bigger room. Stringy was coming out of there after refusing to say much to her, he didn't feel like it ("I don't give a fuck," he said), when the Suit called him.

Where'd he come from? He wore a three-piece suit, which was unusual, but you knew he was Police. "Stringy," he said, "C'mere."

Of course he went. What else can you do?

"Sit down."

Stringy sat.

"How's it going?"

"Okay."

"You got about two years to go, eh? Because of the knife?"

"Yeah."

"You like it here? Some guys like it."

"No."

"Good."

"What's this about, eh?" said Stringy.

"Here." The Suit handed Stringy a Biker magazine, and waited. Stringy opened it up, there was $50 there.

"I don't take no money," said Stringy.

"Jesus — I'm sorry," said the Suit. "Don't know how that got in there. My change this morning, I guess."

The Suit reached out and retrieved the money, folded it into neat little squares and it disappeared.

Stringy looked at the pictures of the Bikes, all big, red Harleys, and pictures of guys having fun at picnics with girls showing their tits. One girl had a butterfly tattooed on her left tit. The Bike roared through a crowd of guys waving beers and the girl with the great tits waved back.

"You like the Bikes, eh?"

"Yeah."

"Ever had one?"

"No."

"Want one?"

"Sure," said Stringy. "Hey — I already talked to the doctor." He thought he might get away with that — he'd pretend this guy was a doctor and he could get out of the room. He knew the guy wasn't. This guy was dealing something. Fuck, you never know . . .

"I don't work here," said the Suit.

"Okay."

"Bikes are nice, eh? On a Bike the world's yours — off you go across the hills, dipping down into curves, nobody can stop you, great — like flying, eh? Next best thing to flying. You ever ride a Harley?"

"No."

"I've had — what — three of them now. Still have a '77 low-rider out in the garage. Jesus — nothing like a Harley. You ride a Harley it's like making love. There's nothing better 'n riding into some quiet little burg with the Bike throttled down to a mean fart, eh? I like that. You park that Bike in front of a tavern and nobody's going to touch it, eh? You walk in for a few beers and all the girls want a ride — you understand me? Classy ladies go for Harleys."

"Fuck," said Stringy.

"I don't work for the prison," the guy said again. "I just came in to visit somebody and saw you going by, thought we should have a talk."

"Yeah?"

"Want to get out early?"

"Sure. Whose cock I got to suck?"

"Hey!" The Suit was pretending to be angry. "Don't talk like that."

"Sorry," said Stringy. You didn't *have* to apologize to Suits — I mean, what the fuck could they do to you that they haven't already done — but sometimes it was a good idea.

"What do you want out of life, Stringy?"

"What do you mean what do I want out of life?"

"That. What do you want to do?"

"Shit. Same as everybody else — have a good time."

"Okay."

"What the fuck's wrong with that?"

"Nothing. Nothing at all. You mean beer?"

"Yeah."

59

"Girls?"

"I ain't no queer."

"Bikes — a Harley?"

"Yeah."

"How are you going to get those things?"

"Fuck — I don't know."

"Sure you do."

"You want me to say I'm going to steal? Shit, I don't know. A lot of guys are in here for trying that, eh?"

"You're not stupid, Stringy."

"No. I ain't stupid."

"You're smarter than most of these guys."

"Yeah."

"You know most of these guys can't read or write, you know that?"

"Yeah."

"You can."

"Yeah. I'm no great hell at it, though."

"You can read that magazine, can't you?"

"Yeah."

"You've got *potential*," said Suit. "Want a job?"

"Doing what? What the fuck's going on?"

"Don't get angry," said Suit. "*You* can't get angry in here, can you? You're still *here*. *You* can't get out. *I* can walk out. I have the Suit. *You* haven't."

"Yeah. Okay."

"Nobody knows I'm here, you know. They let me in, but *they don't know I'm here*. You understand?"

"Yeah."

"You don't do drugs, do you, Stringy?"

"No." (This is what you told them even if you were stoned out of your fucking mind and they knew it.)

"That's good. You got to be quick to survive in this world."

"Yeah."

"You want a Harley?"

"Hey!" Stringy said. "Why are you jerking me around?"

"I'm offering you a Harley."

"Shit. The shit you are!"

"I can deliver, Stringy."

"What the fuck do you want me to do?"

"You want a job?"

"What the fuck you want, eh?"

"You're not leaving, are you, Stringy? I notice you haven't got up to leave. *You* want to leave? You can leave. Nobody is ever going to know you were talking to me. *I'm* not going to tell."

"What's the job?"

"You like Heavy Equipment, eh? Bulldozers? Good money driving a big D-10. Beats stealing."

"Yeah."

"I can get the job for you."

"Yeah."

"Now — I think we should understand one another, Stringy. You're not stupid, are you? I give out the word you're talking to me — and I can — and you're dead meat. You understand me? Dead meat. I'll get the Harley for you. I'll even spring for the leathers. I want you to join a Biker gang and have a good time, drink beer, and play with the ladies' tits and anything else you can get your hands on. There are some pretty classy ladies who just love the Bikers. You can get the tattoos — the whole bit."

"Oh Jesus."

"You're not stupid, are you?"

"Oh Jesus."

"Yeah. I've got you, Stringy. You work for me or I give out that you have — and you're dead meat.

"I'm dead meat if I do!"

"Only if you're stupid. Don't get caught."

"Oh shit, oh Jesus."

"Be tough, Stringy. It's your chance."

"Oh Jesus."

"You want to go now? Okay. Go on, get the fuck out of here. So long as you're alive you'll know I haven't said anything — right? Right? You know what, Stringy? I own your ass. I own your ass, Stringy."

Stringy returned to his cell. His cell-mate (who replaced Willie Jay) had never talked much; now the guy seemed not to talk at all until he said, a week later, "I'm out tomorrow — parole." No warning. Just made the announcement. Fuck! What did that mean?

And then Willie Jay was back.

"What the fuck happened?"

"Ah," grinned Willie Jay, "the god-damned place had a wire straight to the cop shop. Nailed me as I was coming out the door. I'm fucking lucky to be alive."

God, Stringy was glad to see him! God, it was good! God, he was safe! Except how did the Suit get all that stuff about him except from Willie Jay? How come Willie Jay got to come back to his old cell and his old cell-mate. O shit O shit he was being set up.

21

But Willie Jay didn't say fuck and they had a good time sometimes. It was Willie Jay who got the prison artist to give Stringy his first tattoo. Just words: *Born to Lose.* The tattooist suggested the words. Lots of guys wore those words, he said, they were very popular. And Stringy was pleased to have them on his left arm (on his biceps muscle, so the words would show when he rolled up his sleeve for tough work) because they made him feel good, feel loose, feel right, gave him a lively walk the way a good pair of boots give you, which is a damned good thing to feel in prison. A real lift.

Then suddenly it was good-bye to Willie Jay and he was out — fucking bewildered by all the light and space. He drank for a week without leaving Kingston, and bought the services of a couple of dirty girls who asked him about their boyfriends inside. He told them lies. He had nightmares about Bikers mutilating him while he was still alive. He thought what he ought to do was kill Suit, if he could only find the fucker. His prison money was almost gone. Willie Jay said when your number's up your number's up. He wanted to get away. He needed more tattoos, felt cold, needed money to get away from this god-damned place. He was going to have to do a job.

The worst of it was getting the stocking. Shit. If you got caught stealing pantyhose *every*body laughed at you, cops and cons both, and it was no good saying you intended to rob a bank. They just laughed. You might as well cut your throat and be done with it.

But he got the pantyhose out the door of Boots Drugs, heart pounding, safe and back in his grotty little room (shittier than prison), cut them up and tied knots like ears and was ready to go to work.

Pick a branch-bank — that was the word. Willie Jay said *his* weakness was getting pissed and then going for the nearest convenience store — that was stupid, he said. Go for a bank. If you get caught it's the same; if you get away with it it's real money and a rep. Rep is important, eh? You got to have people take you seriously. He even gave Stringy the name of a bank he was kind of saving for himself, but shit, he wouldn't be able to get to it for a while, and by the time he did he figured it would be filled up again, eh? Stringy put the stocking mask over his head and put a piece of metal he'd found by the railway track in his pocket.

If you have a gun it's armed robbery.

At a bank they are not going to shoot you.

In a convenience store or a drug store — BOOM. Shotgun through the guts. You got to be crazy or a druggie to do drug stores or convenience stores.

Me? said Willie Jay. I'm crazy.

Heart pounding through his ears, he couldn't hear a damn thing, Stringy walked into the bank in the town he didn't know from anywhere and gave the note to the princess at the first wicket: GIVE ME ALL THE MONEY. He kept his hand in his pocket with the piece of metal. She was, like, falling out of focus but money came across the counter and she disappeared, probably fainted, and he was sprinting out the door, free, behind the bank, down to a creek bed, walked for fucking miles starting to laugh, threw away the pantyhose mask and the piece of metal first thing and his heart leapt — he wished Willie Jay could see him now, pretty fucking neat, eh?

When he calmed down some he sat down beneath a bridge and got his dick out to think about the princess at the wicket, but nothing doing, he was still too full of triumph, eh? She was a real princess, Willie Jay. Next thing, he was going to get some real tattoos — pictures not just words.

He was walking down the street in Kingston towards the tattoo parlour, he was maybe a block away, when the Suit spoke to him from a parked car. The Suit was sitting there like he'd been waiting for Stringy to come by. Stringy got in the car. "You trying to get me killed?" said Stringy.

"You do all right," said the Suit. "You got away with the bank robbery, didn't you?"

Cold. Cold. Cold. Shit. "What are you talking about?" said Stringy.

"We overlook things if you work for us."

"Oh shit."

"I'm going to give you a number to call. You won't forget it, will you?"

Stringy would try, but he couldn't.

"You've got guts, Stringy," said Suit. "That's what I like about you."

22

You've heard it: tattoos keep you warm. They keep you alive. The blood of the image flows through your veins, and becomes your life — so you take a tiger on your shoulder and you get the tiger's soul. But don't be too quick: that tiger wants to spring, eat, sleep, fuck. You sure you want that? Or do you want a tongue hanging out?

"I sure as shit don't want a *joke* on me!"

Good. Good. This is with you to the grave. It is your mark, your comment, your commitment. People know exactly where you belong. This is your dream. What do you want?

"That one there — *big.*"

How big — big enough to cover your chest — wingtip on your left shoulder? Three colors, going to take some time — but it's a good one. Flight. You ride a bike? This is for somebody who wants to fly free — look, what if I bring the talons down here to clutch your balls. You like that?

"Yes!"

Why?

"I don't know why."

Good. Good. It is good to do what you do not understand. That's what sets us apart, we play with the mysteries, go into the dark, live in dreams.

"And a snake on my arm," said Stringy. "Willie Jay has a bird on his arm and we want to arm wrestle — my snake against his bird, eh? Can you make the snake wrap around my arm so the head is here, eh? — pointing like a fucking pistol? Willie Jay'll shit."

Yes. Yes, I can do that for you. You are going to look very, very good. You are going to be a prize.

23

Fucking Suit thought he was stupid. Fucking Suit thought he had him by the short hairs, that ole Stringy would do whatever Suit wanted because all Suit had to do was break his word to Stringy, and whoever heard of a cop who kept his word, eh? Suit lets the Bikers think Stringy is ratting on them and Stringy will be in a cornfield somewhere begging to die while these Bikers use him for a weenie roast.

But Stringy figured it all out while he was waiting for the tattoos to heal. He got too many too fast, the artist said. He had time to think about things. You ever try to sleep sitting straight up in a chair drunk? Some fucking trick, man. Try it. But God, the tattoos were great! Red Blue Green. He stripped himself naked in front of the mirror and admired himself. He really liked himself when he had a hard-on too and the bird was in flight, like. He laughed — and then shot his snake up at the mirror's throat. "You think that's funny, you fucker? Try this!" And he pinched at the windpipe. Got him.

It was fucking Suit who was dumb. What Stringy was going to do was go back home where there were no Bike Gangs. What about that? How the fuck was he supposed to *inform* on something that wasn't there, eh? Answer me that. Stupid fucker. Want to taste this? Eh? Eh?

24

How were things? Match asked.

Not too bad, Stringy shrugged. He could handle it. He told Match some lies about prison life and Match just ate them up. What an asshole. So far as Match was concerned, Stringy had the truth because he'd done time. And the tattoos, man, were something else! So what was he going to do now? asked Match.

Stringy ignored the question. Where's Trace? he said.

Don't know, said Match. Looney Bin probably.

Yeah. Probably.

It was Match who got him the place to stay, a grotty little room on a grotty street. Tired little houses, all grey. Somebody else got two-years-less-a-day and Stringy got his place full of broken down furniture, empty beer bottles and a TV that didn't work. But there was a full length mirror so he could look at his tattoos while he jacked off. The rest was real down-time. Worse, Match had the idea that because he'd found the place for Stringy and knew him from when they were kids he had some kind of friendship with Stringy. Stringy had to let him know otherwise, so when Match said they should blow this fucking burg Stringy replied (shit, he *had* to) that Match was still alive here, wasn't he? Looked like he was doing pretty good. He was fucking lucky.

Stringy left the clear implication that Match (fatty Match, what a blob) wouldn't last a week in Montreal or Toronto, which was fucking true.

But up in the Mall it wasn't bad; he was a tough guy there because he'd done time in Kingston and the tattoos were widely admired. He wore a Harley T-shirt with the sleeves cut off to show off the snake, especially.

He was sitting by himself on a bench in the Mall outside of Laura Secord when Sharon Branaman and her nice set of tits walked by with her mother. He flashed her a little wave with the snake and you should have seen her eyes pop! She closed up quick like the princess she'd always pretended to be but he knew he'd reached her. He thought she'd probably turn around and glance back at him when she thought it was safe but then the Security Guard was there and said Well, You're Back, and Stringy showed him the snake and said Eat This and the Security Guard said You Just Don't Want an End to Trouble, Do You?

But Stringy did. He caught a glimpse of a Biker in his jacket and recognized the Montreal colors. O shit. Nothing worse. They killed for fun. If they had moved in here he was in deep shit. The guy, he thought, got a glimpse of his Harley T-shirt, too. Fuck! Couldn't he even wear the fucking shirt?

"Hello," said Sharon.

She had come back. He was caught off-guard.

"How are you?" she said.

"Great," said Stringy. "I'm really great." He didn't know what to fucking say.

"Did you think I didn't recognize you?"

"I didn't know," he laughed.

"I have my mother with me — she's up at Holder's Gifts. I wanted to come back to make sure it was really you."

"Well it is," he laughed. "Nobody else."

"What've you been doing?"

"I've been in jail," he grinned. "What about you?"

"I've been working in a bank," she said — and they both laughed. Neat. They balanced.

It was amazing. She just hung around. She didn't sit down — he didn't expect that — but she hung around making talk about the kids they both knew in Grade Seven — Jesus, he'd forgotten all of them. He told her she was discussing Ancient History. It took him a while to realize that what she was doing was cozying up to him, she was inviting him — she was just standing there offering him her great set of tits.

"I can't stay," she said. "I have my mother with me. But I sometimes come up here in the evenings by myself — you know — just to window shop and stuff, around 9 o'clock or so. Maybe we'll run into each other again."

Jesus. She walked off with that proud little tail-twitching walk of hers, but she didn't look back. She might be tempted, but she wasn't going to look back. She wasn't going to let a guy think she was *too* interested in him.

(Some things you learned the hard way. She kept her eyes open for Vincent. She did not want to see him, and his white Corvette was parked outside the mall. With her luck, Vincent would be in Holder's Gifts with his new girl friend talking to her mother. Her mother thought the world of Vincent. Wonder what she'd think if she knew her favorite hair-dresser liked to play stinky-finger with her daughter. Luck — he was nowhere in sight.)

25

"Any luck?" her mother said.

"No," said Sharon.

"Surely they had *Finesse*." (Sharon had told her mother she was going back to Shopper's Drug Mart to look for shampoo when she went back to see if it really was Stringy.)

"Not the size bottle I wanted," said Sharon.

What she ought to do (she thought), was sic Stringy on Vincent. Stringy would scare the shit out of Vincent, and that's what Vincent, smooth Vincent, deserved. What a mistake Vincent had been! But it wasn't her fault; she'd been forced to it. She loved her father, but he was in a way responsible for it, and she let him know it — not about Vincent directly, but indirectly.

"Don't you *care* what happens to me?" she asked her father over the phone.

"Of *course* I care!"

"Then why can't I come to Toronto?"

"It wouldn't be good."

"Why *not*?"

"I can't afford to keep you."

"You've got a girl friend, haven't you," she accused him.

"No I haven't."

She thought he was lying about that. She was sure there was often somebody with him when she telephoned him collect. They telephoned one another often now. The post office box of Stodd Enterprises was for gifts, sometimes a small cheque. Stodd Enterprises was one of her father's jokes. He liked to pretend to be a funny little man named Stodd. She grew tired of that sometimes. And she thought it very unfair of him to condemn her to her mother's life.

But he said she should keep an eye on things.

"What things?" she asked.

"Her future," he said.

Did he mean the house?

"Not only the house," he said. Her future. He wanted her to go to university.

"Why?"

"Because it's necessary for your future."

"I want to come to Toronto to live with you."

"No."

"I can go to high school in Toronto. I can get a job."

"No. Please, Sharon."

She was hurt.

"I liked the photograph you sent me," he said.

"Oh, good." She thought he would. (She thought it was a terrible photograph and hoped he would ask her for something better, different. She looked prissy in it, a year-book photograph and they were all told to wear plain blouses and nothing radical. If they wore anything *radical* or wore radical hairstyles, their pictures would not be used. They might not like the rule, but that was what the rule was. They could take it or leave it.)

"You could come home to me," said Sharon.

"Honey, you know I can't do that."

She did not like him to call her *Honey*. It was something new. But she didn't know how to stop him without hurting his feelings.

"Why not?"

"You know why not . . . Your mother," he said, "could do terrible things. You know that, don't you?"

Yes, she guessed she did. Sharon and her father had formed the unspoken agreement that her mother was so jealous of the affection they shared that she would go to the police and her father would go to jail *even though nothing had happened*. Nothing *has* to happen, he said. All that is needed is someone *saying* something has happened and he would go to jail. She didn't want that, did she?

"No."

"Terrible things happened in prison to men accused of things like that. Killers and bank robbers become their juries, judges, executioners."

She did not want to hear any of this.

"Sharon?"

"Yes."

"Got a boy friend?"

"O Daddy, don't be silly. No."

Although this was not entirely true, it was *mostly* true, until Vincent. Until Vincent there had been the occasional guy she went out with (and perplexed) because she was almost too willing to help him get his rocks off, but she wouldn't fuck, and when he telephoned her later she said no, she "didn't think they should go out again." Sometimes she pretended to have forgotten the guy entirely and he had to introduce himself all over again. Jesus! She got the reputation in high school as a right bitch, a *very* scary girl, the kind to be avoided, probably crazy. I mean, she'd give you a hand-job and wipe your cock off afterwards and then pretend not to remember you. That's scary.

But Vincent got to her, she didn't know why. He was smooth, that was part of it, and he was *not* a student. That mattered. She thought *students* were children. She went to university because it was handy and her father wanted her to, not from any heartfelt desire to make anything special of her life. What she was waiting for was her father to come to some sort of decision about his life; then she'd decide what to do. For example, she told him, if he got married again then she'd decide on her future — but he wasn't even divorced from her mother, was he?

No.

Because *she*, her mother, had not even thought about

73

divorce because she, her mother, thought her father was dead, murdered by Stringy. Once the police got involved her mother *leapt* at the idea that her father had been murdered. Did he know that Stringy was in prison? He was. Tried to hold up a motel in Ontario by knife-point.

"I'm not surprised," said her father.

So she agreed to go to university because her father wanted her to, not for any other reason, and she would do the work required because she was good at whatever she wanted to do — didn't he know that?

Why didn't the two of them go into business? They could have their own boutique. She'd be good at that.

"The commercial world is dog-eat-dog."

"You're doing okay."

"Arf-Arf," he said, and she laughed.

But she had been really irritated with her father the day she happened to meet Vincent. That was a bad day, she now realized.

Her father should have thought about the effect his constant rejection was having *on her*.

She and a couple of girls from that stupid introductory Anthropology class — the girls were from out of town and didn't know anything about Sharon's local reputation — were in Dooby's bumping down a beer and this dark-haired guy came over to talk to Eileen, Sharon wasn't even listening until he turned to her and said, "Come on — let's go for a drive."

He didn't give her a chance to say no. He held out his hand and took her out to his car, which was a white Corvette. She liked settling herself into it, flashing her legs, smoothing her skirt, and he said something which said a great deal about him and just how shallow he really was. He said, smiling, "Life's a movie."

But she didn't know how shallow he was then; she thought he was "interesting." He was that rare creature (he said), a heterosexual hair dresser. In fact, it turned out that he did her mother's hair. Sharon asked him what he thought of her mother. Vincent said her mother was quiet — and had nice soft hair, although not so nice, and not so soft, as her daughter's. Ooooooo, said Sharon. They enjoyed mocking each other then. Vincent said he was married, but separated. He had fallen into one of those teen-age traps and getting out of it was hell. Had she fallen into a trap like that?

"No."

"Good for you," Vincent said.

Vincent himself had really nice dark hair, perfectly smooth. Mediterranean ancestry, he said. His grandmother didn't speak English. 100% Greek. He loved his grandmother, visited her often. Old Greek lady dressed entirely in black. You see her out walking in winter and you think Death has come to fetch you.

Vincent had never bothered finishing high school. He went into hair dressing because it was a good business and he was good at it and (he smiled) he liked women. He wasn't doing badly. He had a chain of salons — well, three parlors. You work a percentage deal with the hairdressers but you take the lease and run the show. He was thinking about franchising.

Sharon liked the idea of Vincent doing her mother's hair in the morning and playing with Sharon on the waterbed in the afternoon. And she really did think they looked good together. She told him one afternoon on the waterbed she loved him and he told her he could love her, too, although he could not exactly reciprocate because of his marriage situation. She should have known then, but she was crazy in love with him. You could ask anyone. Although she couldn't tell her mother about Vincent, that was pretty obvious, wasn't it.

She felt in a way she had betrayed her father, but she had

75

her own life to think about and in a way it was her father's fault for *not doing anything*. Now that Stringy was back her father would have another excuse for not coming home. She decided not to tell him about Stringy. And Vincent had very nearly ruined her life. She trembled when she thought of how she had dropped out of university for him. Yes she *had*! He didn't have to believe that if he didn't want to, but he certainly expected a woman who accompanied him to *look good*, and to look good she needed clothes. How could she buy clothes and go to university both?

So for *his sake* she went to her mother and said she had decided university was not worth it, what did it get you anyway? She wasn't going to pretend she found it exciting. She thought she'd get a job for a while.

Her mother was predictably outraged because her mother had paid the tuition.

"I'm not *failing*," said Sharon. "Would you like to see the marks on my essays? I'm not even *trying* and I'm making B's. I write these on my way to class. So I *can* do it — I just don't want to. It's stupid."

"Well, what about the tuition?"

"I'll pay you back."

"O you will, will you?"

"Yes."

And her mother was all set to leap into the Failure lecture — "You'll end up a waitress!" — which her mother thought was a fate worse than death (and in fact Sharon agreed with her although she wouldn't say so, she had no intention of *ever* waiting on tables), but Sharon topped her. She'd been waiting for this moment.

"I've got a job."

"Where?"

"In the bank."

"You haven't!"

76

"Why are you always calling me a liar!?"

"I can't believe it."

"Well you'd better — because I start Monday."

And she did. It was a good, respectable job, handling money. It required skill and good manners — and nice clothes. She had to dress well. She liked having the job, although she couldn't say she cared much for doing it, even though she seemed to be very good at it. She'd been doing it now for two years, and earning what could only be called a pitiful little salary. "What we should do," she remarked to one of her co-workers, "is work on commission."

That was the kind of remark that got you stared at. She didn't care. They all took this terribly seriously. She didn't.

And her mother never found out about Vincent. That was a triumph. Two years of Vincent and her mother never found out. Her mother would have had a fit if she had known how many afternoons Sharon spent spread naked on Vincent's waterbed while he did whatever he wanted to with her.

26

Vincent said: "It's over."

"What?"

He was sorry, but . . .

"Over?"

He was sorry, but times were hard. He was going bankrupt. He didn't want to tell her, but he was going bankrupt.

She told him she didn't believe him, but she knew what she did believe: he had something going on with his so-called franchisee. "You should see the look on your face!" she told him.

"You don't understand what I'm talking about," he said. "Bankrupt." He spelled it out for her. And it was partly her fault, too.

"*My* fault?"

"Yeah, your fault. Christ, the *attention* you demand, the jesus phone calls. How'm I supposed to pay attention to business?"

"My fault? What about that lumpy little slut?"

"Look — let's just say we made a mistake, eh?"

"You shit," she said.

Then she saw him walking around with that lumpy little slut *with the henna hair* from across the river and she knew that he was just mocking her, that he was an absolute coward.

Sharon made a couple of phone calls to the new girl and made her cry. That was something. The third time Vincent was on the line saying this call was being taped and if she called again the police would be informed. "Your mother will know," said Vincent, the smug bastard!

Since then she hadn't been able to do a thing. But

everywhere she went she looked for him, thought of revenge, of how badly she'd been treated. She hoped he lost
every god-damned cent and she couldn't understand how,
if he was going bankrupt, he kept the white Corvette.

27

It was not that Lorraine was quiet — she was tired.

That was the truth of the matter. It was unfair of Sharon
to complain that her mother was uncommunicative. Why
should she be expected to be cheerful after a day of doing
menial work for the mind? Yes, she'd heard that phrase and
it fit. You picked up a file-folder and you put it in the
drawer under the correct letter of the alphabet; the phone
rang and you did it again. Dress it up any way you will, it
came to that. She'd been doing it for some twenty years
now — a job which seemed "a start," once, and "handy,"
later, but now — a "career woman" against her will — a
life. Not a *career*; a terrible *job*. A terrible life. She counted

up her sick days and made sure she used every one of them. She wasn't going to give them a bit more than was required of her.

Of course she was pleasant and polite, always civil. She was that kind of person. She did not like the part of the job that required her to collect urine specimens, but she did it. Did Sharon have any understanding of what that meant? A dirty old farmer handed her a vial of his urine. She had to take it, deal with it, label it, pass it on. She held her breath. You just think about that for a while, young lady. It is not a life I'd wish on anyone, but I've stuck with it. What choice did I have — after I lost my husband? Do you really think women *choose* careers? They "choose" careers because they have no choice.

Quiet? No. I'm tired.

28

They were in her mother's car at the gravel pit because she told Stringy he could take her anywhere he wanted to, life was a movie, wasn't it?

Hey, he said, for sure.

Stringy wanted to talk about prison, and she let him. She thought his stories were really fascinating. The only way you could survive a mean fucker like Gagnon, he said, was to be meaner than he was. You *got* mean in prison — then you got out and it's hard to change your ways. That's why so many guys end up going back.

"You?"

"I'm not going back alive," he said.

He had a bottle of rye and they took turns swigging from it.

"Bet you never thought you'd end up drinking with an ex-con in a gravel pit, did you?" he said.

"Bet you never thought I'd like it, did you?" she said.

They seemed to make one another laugh. She made the first move. She scooted over to him — he was on the driver's side (she let him drive, of course, that pleased him) — and kissed him on the neck while he was pulling from the bottle.

"Jesus, you'll make me spill this."

"Then you'll have to take off your clothes, won't you?" she said.

Jesus, he was stunned. "You . . . you . . . just want to see my tattoos," he laughed. "You heard about my tattoos."

"You have more than the snake?"

"Yep. I've got more than the snake."

He coiled the snake around her neck and she kissed its

head on his hand and then kissed his mouth, then kissed him again using her tongue quickly. "Snake-kiss," she said. "Snake-kiss." She rubbed herself up against him, those beautiful tits. He put his hands on them and she made a soft little sound of agreement and kissed him with a lot of tongue action. Then she pulled away and unbuttoned her blouse, took it off, and her bra, threw it in the back seat. "We can be a bit more comfortable," she said.

Stringy caressed her bare tits, he was dizzy with triumph, this was more than he had ever imagined while talking with Willie Jay.

She pushed him away gently. "I'm so hot," she said softly. She was moving her hips. "Do I get to see the other tattoos?"

They got out of the car and he tugged off his shirt. There wasn't much light — all she could make out was the outline of the wings of the tattoo, the suggestion of the dark head. She wanted to put her hands on it, she said, and did — hands all over his tattoo, hands all over his back. When she found the Tiger on his shoulder she kissed it, driving him wild. He was afraid he was going to come in his pants, and that would be terrible, embarrassing. He unzipped.

She shocked him by going down on her knees immediately and taking his cock in her mouth. He was trembling, trying not to come.

Then she stood up, unzipped her jeans, peeled them down with her panties and stepped out of them, kicked off her sandals. She bent over the fender of the car and waggled her beautiful white ass. "Can you take me like this?" she asked.

He did — but o shit he came too quick, shit — but jesus he'd been holding it back so fucking long, for fucking ever. But she made sounds like she was ready for it and when he pulled away and she turned around, jesus! she went down on him again all greasy, just for a bit, because she wanted it all, she said. Then they got back in the car naked and drank quite a bit, he more than she. He had never been so happy or so nervous in his life. He had a silly little laugh.

"Jesus, I'm glad I ran into you," he said.

"Me too," she said. Then, soberly: "I think somehow we were *fated* to come back together. I never forgot you, Stringy. And what my father did to you." She looked at him like she was torn apart. "I think you own me, I really do."

Jesus.

29

She meant it when she said it, she knew she did, she really did. She hadn't *planned* to fuck Stringy at all, it had just happened, all she'd planned to do was see him for a while, maybe tell him he didn't have to worry about her father, but she'd thought better of that.

But when you stopped to think about it afterwards (she was quite sober; she would tell her mother she and a few of the girls from the bank went out for a drink, was there anything wrong with that? you couldn't say there was anything wrong with that, could you?), it was all pretty ridiculous. All those tattoos! She'd never seen anything like those tattoos. It was like he was with a circus or something!

And O my, the things she said! Embarrassing.

Maybe she would get Stringy to kill her mother.

My God, what a thought! Don't be silly.

30

Her mother was complaining about not feeling well, a "frothing in her stomach," but Sharon wasn't interested. She was suspicious of her mother's illnesses. She was more interested in the flyer she found on the hall table.

"What's this?" she wanted to know.

"Nothing," said her mother, as if casually. "Just a flyer." A pause. "She said someone wants to buy our house."

"*Who* said?"

"The realtor. The real estate woman."

"You have no right!" shouted Sharon. "No right!" (The real estate woman even had a little picture of herself in the flyer. The *gall* of the woman! Smooth. Butter wouldn't melt in her mouth.)

Her mother tried to explain. The woman — the realtor — just dropped by to say that she had some American clients who were re-locating here and they were driving by and said "that's the house we want," so she, the real estate woman, had come by to ask if perhaps they were interested, she didn't want to pressure them at all, just inquiring.

"Oh sure."

"She was just inquiring."

"It's my home too!"

31

Lorraine could not sell the house even if she wanted to (she had no idea where the deed was), but she liked to have the opportunity. Nobody knew what a *burden* this house was. The care it took. When the furnace broke down that time and the trouble she had getting it fixed; she was sure she was cheated on the bill. If Lee came back one day it would serve him right to find it a charred, burnt-out shell, tattered curtains billowing out through empty windows. (She imagined the scene in winter; Lee would be tramping through the snow in his street-shoes because he was too vain to wear galoshes; big boys didn't wear galoshes, he said.) It was the not-knowing that wore her out.

The police? They knew more than they would tell her, she thought, and she especially resented their evasions because she had not wanted to go to the police in the first place. The principal of Lee's school, good old Ginger, had insisted. They would not even tell her if they thought he was dead. She found it difficult to imagine him dead, but she wanted to *know*. How was she to go on with her life if she did not *know*? Sharon did not seem to understand it was the not-knowing that was so exhausting. Sharon said fiercely that she *always* had hope, that she would not allow her mother to *kill* her father. Oh, it just made her stomach hurt.

She asked the wavey-haired detective the question point-blank: "Is he dead?"

"We just don't know," the detective said. But he *had* to say that, didn't he? They couldn't find him. The detective tried to deflect her from her purpose by asking insulting questions — as if they would make her go away.

Could she think of any "personal reasons" Lee might have had for leaving?

What kind?

Private reasons.

She refused to respond and stood in front of the detective's desk until he came out with it. "Did he have a lady friend somewhere?"

"No," she said. She would have known. She threw her mind back over their life together. He was not out often in the evenings, nor mysteriously. There had never been the smell of another woman on him. Whatever his failings, Lee Branaman had never been guilty of *that*.

"Boy friends?"

That's what she meant by insulting questions meant to drive her away. She refused to respond — and the detective, in turn, refused to take seriously the possibility that the boy Lee had punished his last day at school might have been responsible.

"He's too small," said the detective.

"He could have used a gun," she said.

The detective didn't think so. They had no reason to suspect this boy, he said. They were continuing their enquiries. (The police did not know that Stringy had been arrested and imprisoned in Ontario, although Sharon did — she heard the news at Dooby's and passed it on to her father in the vain hope he might feel it safe to come home now — but that would mean her father would have to come back to her mother, and she could see why he would not want to do so. She was on the point of asking her father if she was to wait until her mother died — but thought better of it. Nor did she tell her mother that she knew Stringy was in prison. It was just one of those things she did not want her mother to know.)

What the police did not tell Lorraine — there was no reason to, unless something turned up — was that they had looked very hard for Lee Branaman's car. They had most certainly discussed the matter with Gibby. They'd made him lock those god-damned dogs in an ancient milk-delivery truck and they had checked every wreck on his disgusting lot. Nothing. That told you a great deal — because a man can disappear more easily than a Lincoln Continental. What they thought they'd find, a couple of years down the line, was that the Lincoln Continental had been sold in Toronto, and the seller was none other than Lee Branaman.

But to Lorraine they had to say nothing had turned up, their enquiries were continuing.

She returned to a house which was an agony every time she entered it. It boomed with echoes of her broken heart, she thought, especially after she returned from the police station — as if each visit merely confirmed what she feared most. The house was a nightmare of constant reproach, endless chambers of vast emptiness.

32

When Sharon telephoned her father she sometimes found him edgy, and not as attentive as she hoped and expected. She had the feeling that sometimes there was someone else there with him, but he always denied it. He was pleased with her, however, for getting the deed to the house out of the safe-deposit box. "Good girl," he said. It was no trick, she replied. She had access to the vault, of course, and he had sent her the key to the safe-deposit box. She was in there and out with the deed in a moment — frightened while doing it, of course, but proud and triumphant. Her mother would never know. She'd bring the deed with her when she came to Toronto.

Came to Toronto? This was new.

Well — yes. But she wanted to. She wanted to see him. It was *unbearable*, this. She didn't know how much longer she could stand to . . . you know, be apart from him, knowing he was there. She had to see him.

Well, he laughed, soon. But not now. He didn't want her to see him until he had improved his life a little. A shoe salesman, for god's sake! Think about what that meant! She could imagine, couldn't she? Bent over people all day. Kneeling at their feet! As if waiting to be knighted! Maybe she should wait until he received his knighthood.

She knew he was putting her off, and she was not happy, and let him know it by the tone of her voice.

33

Angela was not eavesdropping, but it was a small apartment, and she could not help but know something from the tone of his voice as he talked on the phone in the next room.

"Your daughter?" she said, when he came back.

"Yes," he said. "How did you know?"

"I'm intuitive," she said.

Angela was forty and forthright; chunky but attractive; a bit overweight but well-groomed. She was the executive assistant to a provincial cabinet minister. They met when Lee sold her a pair of shoes.

"Nice fit," he said, slipping the pump on her foot. The sound was neat, and with the right words in the right tone to refer to it, quite suggestive.

She took his meaning. "Hard to find," she said — and then laughed loudly to show that she was a lively, up-front woman. "You want to take me out to dinner?" she said. "I'll pay for the drinks the first time."

Lee was taken aback. "You didn't ask if I was married," he said.

"I don't care," she said. There was a bit of revenge in her attitude, it turned out. Her ex-husband had been fooling around with a married woman when she caught him. She blamed the woman. From then on she decided to look out for Number One, herself, and Number Two, her twelve-year-old son. Okay?

And what she liked about Lee was his flashiness. She liked his big, old rich-man's car and his flashy shoes. They looked like golfing shoes, she said. He seemed kind of dramatic. She didn't like hum-drum.

What she had decided about him was that he was an executive who had been fired for some kind of malfeasance, maybe using inside information on the stock exchange, maybe even embezzlement. Maybe he had gone to jail. Black-listed, of course. That was why he was selling shoes. There was a story, she figured, behind every shoe-salesman.

And she didn't mind a little danger. She knew when to get out, and how. She'd learned a lot, she thought bitterly, from her ex-husband.

"You're not really a shoe-salesman, are you?"

"Sure I am."

"No. That's not you."

"What I am," he said, "is that I don't give a shit. Okay?"

"Yes," she said. "Good." That suited her just fine. He wasn't the greatest guy in the world — he wasn't all that great in bed, for example — but on the other hand, he wasn't permanent, either. They went to his place from time to time. Never to hers.

34

It was not fair. Too much was being expected of her, and there were too few rewards. She was *not* going to be sorry to leave the bank. (She had decided to go to Toronto; she would tell her father when she would be arriving, and he wouldn't *dare* not meet her!) And Stringy — Stringy was becoming a problem. Some of the things she had said and done were mistakes. She could admit that to herself. But boys took these things so seriously — when it suited them, of course. Vincent had been just as serious as *he* wanted to be. But Stringy . . . well, by going to Toronto she would solve the awkward problem of Stringy, too.

An awkwardness demonstrated by Stringy's decision to have the *serious talk*. Boys always wanted to have the *serious talk*.

Stringy began: "I'm in deep shit, Sharon."

She did not want to hear this. What it meant was that, somehow or other, she was to get him out of deep shit.

"They own my ass."

"They?"

"When I was in the pen I shared a cell with a guy named Willie Jay — you've heard me talk about him. Well, I thought he was a good guy, a really good guy, I liked him, we got along, laughed and joked. Shit! We even jacked off together, that's how close we were."

He closed his eyes as if he were in a trance; this was terrible.

"But the police, the Mounties," he said, "Shit — I don't even know who, all I've got is a fucking number, got to Willie Jay or something or they got something on him and he must have told them about me to get them off his back

— they're such shits, the police, you wouldn't believe what shits they are — and so this one cop gets me and says to me that he wants me to join a Biker Gang and become an Informer."

He turned to look at her; he looked terrible.

"They kill you if they find out," he said. "They don't give a shit, they chop people up, they don't give a fuck about anything."

"Oh, Stringy." (Who was he talking about?)

"I'm scared, Sharon. What it is, see — if I don't inform, the cops tell them I *have* — and it comes out the same — they kill me."

"O my God," she said. She didn't understand how it was that he was going to be killed. But she could understand his terror easily enough.

"I came back to this fucking town because there are no Biker Gangs here — I mean, there are connections, but there's no Clubhouse, eh? And because you're here," he added.

"Oh, Stringy," she said. But she couldn't quite believe that the police were out to get him killed. Was that what he meant? That didn't seem likely. All he had to do was stay out of trouble.

"I'm scared, Sharon."

Why was he *telling* her all this? She didn't want to know. Why was he dumping all this on her? Did she tell *him* her problems? It wasn't fair. "You poor darling," she said. Why was it you always had to give *sympathy* to men — her father, Vincent, now Stringy. It wasn't fair.

But there was worse to come. He was beginning to smile. He had plans. Plans which, it seemed, involved her. Ludicrous plans. Dreams. Something about a heavy-equipment course at some community college or other. Getting off Welfare.

"Being on Welfare means never having enough to do

what you want," he explained. He was clearly proud of the thought.

They'd get out of this place; move on. They could live in a mobile home . . .

Mobile home!

And she could work in a bank somewhere while he was taking this heavy equipment course.

"Oh, Stringy — let's just enjoy ourselves, right now."

She began to unbuckle his trousers.

But he was angry. "No!"

This was serious, he said. He raised his chin. He wouldn't look at her; it was that serious. "I love you, Sharon," he said. "Never said that to anybody."

"Oh Stringy," she said — and kissed him. She was *not* going to say she loved him, too, just because he said it. That was another expectation. Men did that.

But he took the kiss as . . . what? Encouragement? Agreement? He was smiling again; he was happy.

"I want you to get a tattoo for me," he said.

She was stunned. She was proud of being unmarked. But she laughed briefly. "A butterfly on my hip?" she suggested, as if she were going to consider it.

But no. Worse.

"I'll get your name tattooed on my hand where everybody can see it," he said. "I want you to get my name tattooed on your tit. Little heart and my name, eh? Little red heart and my name."

It was all she could do to keep from laughing. STRINGY? Did he want LOVE on the other?

35

Fuck. They wanted fucking Grade Twelve or equivalency before they would let him take Heavy Equipment. Fucking sorry but that's the way it is. And fuck, he had been totally honest with Sharon and it didn't make any fucking difference.

Oh, she'd *put out*. All he had to do was unzip and she'd be down there with some sweet tongue action without him saying a word — but it didn't seem to *matter* to her. She'd finish and say, "You feel better?" as if he was fucking sick or something.

Fuck. If she really loved him she'd get a tattoo. You spilled your guts and what did it get you? Nothing.

She said it was really bad news about the Heavy Equipment course. Life wasn't fair. She'd brought a bottle. Maybe that would make him feel better. She said she'd had some news which was . . . unsettling.

"Your father?"

"What? No." No, the news was that she was being promoted.

"Hey, Great."

Well, not so great. The catch was that she had to go to Toronto.

"I don't want to go to Toronto," he said. "I'll get killed there."

That's what she meant. It wasn't all good news. She didn't really have a choice.

"What do you mean . . . don't have a choice."

"No choice," she said. Either she took the promotion and went to Toronto or they let her go.

What the fuck was she trying to say to him? The answer was simple enough. Tell them to shove it up their ass. She could stay here, get another job.

She said she had to go.

No she didn't.

"Yes."

"No! God-damn it."

"Stringy," she said . . . "Circumstances."

"Fuck circumstances."

That was no answer, she said, smiling. Little smile. Satisfied smile.

"All right," he said. "I'm sorry about the tattoo. No tattoo. Okay?"

She smiled and kissed him. But he pushed her away. He wanted to get things clear. All right? Clear. She was not fucking going to Toronto.

She was sorry. She was really sorry. Sorrier than she could tell him. But she had to go. Really.

No.

She went for his belt-buckle, and he pushed her back, back-handed her across the face. NO!

She started to cry.

"I'm sorry," he said. "Jesus I'm sorry."

"I can't help it, Stringy. I can't help it. I don't want to go but I have to." She wept. She said she couldn't stop weeping. She shook with sobs.

"I'll rob the fucking bank," he said.

She gave a little laugh. That wouldn't do any good.

"I'll rob it. See if I don't."

"What good will that do?"

"You can't leave me!"

"Stringy — be reasonable."

"I'll rob the fucking bank!"

And then — god-damn her, she just got in her mother's car and drove off. Just like that. Just like fucking that. He

96

meant nothing to her and he loved her so much it was driving him crazy. You spill your guts, and what does it get you?

36

Her mother was whining about the way Sharon treated her, expecting Sharon to arrange her life around her mother's convenience in small domestic matters of no significance whatever, and complaining about her health, something "gnawing at her," she felt something was "gnawing at her insides."

"Cancer?" suggested Sharon. That was cruel.

It was very cruel, her father said, responding to Sharon. They were talking on the phone. There was no point in being cruel.

But he didn't *know*, thought Sharon. He didn't know what her mother was like. He had his life in Toronto, and didn't have to live with the poisonous woman, always whining. Sharon was bitter. "Maybe she's going to die?" she suggested. "What then?"

He said he wouldn't wish that on anyone — and Sharon understood that he was happy, someone was making him happy, and she was being shut out of his life, some woman with dyed black hair and many, many sparkling rings was doing anything he wanted and was just waiting to be introduced to Sharon, cooing "So this is your *daughter* — I've heard so much about you." I'll bet.

The evidence was clear. He was now talking about "going places." You don't "go places" alone. Centre Island. Fouled with goose shit, he said.

Sharon said she was going to surprise him one of these days.

"What do you mean by that?"

"Oh — you'll find out," she sang, laughing.

"No, seriously — what do you mean?"

New words. He'd never said anything like that before: *No, seriously.* He'd picked that up from the woman with the dyed black hair. He was changing, slipping away, and she could not always remember exactly what he looked like now, and had begun to give herself a task: memorizing the sizes of all his clothes. She made herself say the list several times a day.

"Do you still wear the same size shoes?"

"Of course," he laughed. "Feet don't change."

He didn't used to laugh about things like that.

"I'm coming to Toronto," she said.

"Sharon — no."

Sharon no! "Flight 643. Next Thursday. Meet me."

She hung up the phone, furious.

37

Sharon said she could *not* talk to him, please do *not* call her on the telephone, she might be at Tim Horton's this evening if she could get away, she'd do what she could but no promises, *shit*! He smashed the telephone receiver against the box and the box cracked like ice giving way and the receiver broke in fucking two. Hey! Great! But then there was a cop car turning the corner (how do they fucking *know?*), and he was off through the parking lot, *god-damn her*, into the back lot of Geezer's, he could hear the cop car doors thumping closed, *god-damn her! she had no right, no right*, fuck fuck fuck, he was at the fence of the Honda dealer's so what the fuck he leapt at it and climbed it, right up the fucker, over the top, cut his hand, shit who gives a fuck and into the lot. Ha Ha Ha Ha Ha. Ha Ha Ha.

There was a bike there in the lot. He looked around. He was alone inside the fenced-in lot. He went over and straddled the bike. Jap Junk. Nipon shit. He'd cut his hand, shit. Blood. He kicked at the bike, it turned over but didn't catch. It wasn't locked. Hey! He kicked it again. He'd be off and away except how the hell did he expect to get it out of the fucking enclosure? Fly it? Shit. Shit, shit, shit. He was being mocked. And here came some lights, a car. Fuck. The cops. He had to go up and over the fucking fence again and jesus his hand hurt! The bastards! *God-damn them, God-damn her.* Look at my tattoos. Have a good look, you Fuckers! Yeah, you. Fuckers! Cocksuckers!

38

But there was worse.

Two days later he was in Tim Horton's drinking coffee when a cop sat down on one side of him and his partner cop sat down on the other side of him and they started talking to one another right fucking *through* him, talking about the silly shit who tried to steal a broken motorcycle which was in for repair at the Honda dealer's. The silly shit, they agreed, probably expected to *fly* over the fence or slither under it, probably high on something or other, or sniffing glue like a kid. They knew who it was, of course, no problem at all. The guy acted like a Retard.

Stringy had to sit there and take it. They were just egging him on. They wanted him to cause a disturbance so they could have the excuse of hauling him in and putting the boots to him and putting him back in prison where the Bikers could get at him and he'd be dead in three days hanging from his belt in his fucking cell. He had to sit there and take it while they drank their fucking coffee slow.

Fuckers. They didn't know it was Welfare Day. They left, he got his cheque and went on a three-day drunk.

39

Cancer. The dreaded word. Lorraine was glad that Sharon had said it. You would expect it from Sharon. And she was almost certainly right. The gnawing at her insides, knives cutting her up inside, pain shooting through her bowels that drove her to her knees quite literally in private, in the house, when Sharon wasn't there. In public Lorraine clenched her teeth and stood still, enduring the pain while it wracked through her.

The doctor's receptionist was anything but co-operative on the telephone. She would not, first, allow Lorraine to speak to the doctor, and, second, insisted on knowing the symptoms of her discomfort. When Lorraine said she wished to discuss them with the doctor, the receptionist said, "I'm a Nurse."

"I'm dying," said Lorraine. "No one knows."

"Lorraine?" said the nurse. "Lorraine?"

"What?"

"Is that you, Lorraine? From Nurses' Training? VPH? Way back when?" (Ah, she had just remembered that Lorraine had not finished. Did she remember why?) "This is Marilyn. Remember? Marilyn Mack."

"Yes."

"Are you okay?"

"Yes."

"What a silly thing to say," laughed Marilyn. "You wouldn't be calling if you were okay, would you?"

"No," Lorraine laughed, too. "No I wouldn't."

(There were two kinds of nurses. Lorraine knew. She had known then and had confirmed it since at the hospital. There were those who, like Lorraine, wanted to do something useful with their lives. Lorraine had had every intention of going to Africa to be a missionary nurse. *Yes she had*! That was what she meant to do. Lee ruined her life with Sharon. All those little happy black children and their grateful mothers she could have helped! And the golden sunlight on the clearing, the thatched huts, the heat — she would have made them happy and they would have infected her with their happiness. She used to smile. *Yes she did*!)

But the doctor told her, days later, that there was nothing wrong. The tests showed nothing wrong.

Nothing wrong?

Why were they lying to her? Everyone was lying to her.

"Good news, eh?" smiled Marilyn.

And Lorraine was forced to do the expected thing and smile and lie in return. "Yes, it certainly is. It's quite a relief." She had to lie and lie and lie. She was sick of it.

40

Not many things that a man could do, compared to what her ex-husband had done (stolen her car, and wrecked it), could upset Angela, but she was annoyed when she heard Lee telling lies to his daughter on the telephone. She felt as if Lee were somehow deceiving her as well. So when he popped out to get another bottle one Saturday afternoon, she had a quick look around his apartment, and found a letter from his daughter written six or seven years ago at the bottom of his sock-drawer.

The letter upset her — and she decided that she'd better ease herself out of this relationship as quickly and delicately as she could and make him think it was his idea because — oh hell, you know how it is, telephone calls late at night, stuff like that.

41

Dear Daddy,

I love you, I love you.

Yours sincerely (ha, ha)

Sharon E. Branaman

P.S. I *mean* it!

NO ERRORS

42

What surprised people about Sharon Branaman was that she was very good at what she did: she did not make mistakes. At the end of a sweaty day when the other tellers were hoping against hope that everything would tally — and then hoping that the mistake would not be too difficult to find — Sharon sat with her hands in her lap waiting for quitting time. It was almost uncanny — and it was difficult not to think about promoting her except that she did not get along especially well with the other girls. Nothing you could put your finger on exactly, but she was *flip*; she might have a smart remark or she wouldn't answer you at all. She didn't seem to care about anything in the world. She had a terrible pride.

Well, that was *partly* true — Sharon would admit that. She did *not* talk about husbands and babies and houses all the time the way the others did. But they were married. Sharon didn't like them for that alone. If anybody had asked her what she wanted out of life she would have replied without thinking: I want what is rightfully mine; nothing more, nothing less. Vincent was behind her. Vincent had taught her a harsh lesson about delusion. Stringy was pretty exotic — with his tattoos, his criminal past — but he was not someone you took seriously. Stringy did not count.

But she did not think of him as a truly terrible error (Vincent had been a truly terrible error!) until she saw Stringy in the line-up of the bank and realized that he was very, very drunk, and might very well make a terrible, terrible scene — "Come back to me, please, don't leave me" — and, after the awful silence, there might well arise some confusion over the two stories she had told to explain her sudden, impending departure from the bank. (To the bank personnel officer she had explained that a place had suddenly become available in an airline flight attendant training program, and that it had long been a dream of hers, and so on, and the class started in one week in Toronto. She liked the idea of herself in a neat uniform with a red scarf at her neck, smiling at businessmen.)

She would pretend not to know him.

She kept her head down, as if she had not seen him. She was supposed to open her station, but she'd stall, go back to the vault for $20s or something, she *would not participate*.

But Stringy ignored the girl he should have gone to, and went straight for Sharon instead. His face was drunk, he didn't care about anything in the world, and he frightened her. She held her breath and let the dizziness rise through her, shutting off thought.

Then he gave her the note and she read it and had to read it twice before she realized that he was holding-up the bank, just like he promised.

Because there were certain transactions which had to be okayed by Anne Purvis, she took the note to Anne. Stringy followed her, went crazy, banged Anne Purvis's head up and down on the desk — and the blood, oh, the blood spattering, ruining things. The ruin was terrible, and she was annoyed with Stringy for trying to ruin things, she hated him, she . . .

Stringy was out the door and she was safe. Nothing had happened. She was safe.

43

Sharon put her mother's car keys on the hall table. Her mother was ironing clothes in the dining room again, which irritated Sharon. There was no need to iron every evening, for one thing — although her mother disputed this, saying she did not want a load to pile up and overwhelm her.

And for another thing, Sharon thought it was tacky to iron in the dining room. Why not use one of the empty rooms on the top floor?

Because, her mother said when she suggested it, *you* don't have to carry the laundry all the way up there.

Sharon stood listening to her mother's work: thud, hiss, thud, hiss. Her mother hadn't even called out to ask who it was. She was punishing Sharon for something, probably for coming in so late.

Sharon displayed herself in the doorway, inviting her mother to say something — here I am, as if to say, What do you want to say to me?

Nothing? Then I have nothing to say to you, either.

Sharon went to bed.

44

Angela was touched; it was a very nice dinner at an Italian restaurant off Yonge Street. Lee was making a real effort. It was a pity that he was the wrong sort for her life. She wasn't going to think any farther, that was far enough. She was tired of wrong men.

After the meal was over he looked at her with a confident smile, as if he were going to offer her a ring — which he couldn't, of course.

But what he did offer was worse: a copy of his lawyers' letter to his wife, requesting a divorce. When Angela had finished reading the letter, Lee said: "My wife already has it — the letter, I mean. It was mailed out day before yesterday." He was proposing to her.

He was so pleased with himself. She felt his need sucking her in, drawing her into the mess of his life. That daughter. This is how women married killers, she thought. You got sucked into somebody's need.

"I hope you didn't do that for me," she said. And then, immediately (but too late), "I'm sorry — that sounded terrible, didn't it."

But she meant what she said, and stuck to it, politely but firmly, she thought. Lee paid the bill and outside the restaurant just walked away from her, didn't even look back at her. She was sorry for that, but it was for the best, it really was. She hoped he wouldn't pester her with calls. She had to take a taxi home. What Lee would never have thought of was that she had to consider her son as well as herself. He had never given a thought to Tommy, she knew that. Men never did; they think only of themselves.

45

Lorraine hobbled away from the heavy old door unable to understand why a Toronto law firm would be sending her a heavy letter, and when she read it, still in the hall, she shrieked and felt the house torn apart. Everything gone! A terrible darkness.

Her husband wished to obtain a divorce. It was hoped that an amicable division of property might be achieved.

She had been betrayed, betrayed!

Wouldn't Sharon lord it over her now!

Wouldn't she love to see her mother turned out into the street!

Betrayed!

She marched upstairs to have it out with Sharon and kicked at her door. It was always locked, but now flew open. Open. Had it been locked? It was open and available to her.

"Sharon!"

Nothing.

There was an opportunity.

It was a trap.

"Sharon?"

46

Match had sniffed so much glue that his head was fucking hollow. He wore this army shit, tiger clothes to make him look like a jungle-fighter. What an asshole. But he had this survival knife.

"Gimme it."

"Why?"

"Because I'm fucking desperate," said Stringy. So Match gave him the knife. Stringy said he needed food, too.

What kind of food.

McDonald's, Burger King, I don't care. Get me a couple of Big Macs. Match said he didn't have any money so Stringy gave him his last folding bill, a five dollar bill, which meant that he didn't have any money in his jeans but the coins in his god-damned pocket. Then he waited all night on the school playground before he realized that fucking Match wasn't going to come back. That did it. Fucking Match should know the rules.

Match was history.

He was going to kill Match with his own fucking knife.

Match was dead meat.

47

He hid out down by the river clutching himself to keep warm but he found a big piece of plastic which had blown away from a construction site so he had shelter and some moments he thought he could hide out here for fucking ever, the stupid cops would never find him, but he needed food and had probably better get out of town. So he used his last god-damned quarter to telephone Sharon from a pay phone and told her to get her mother's car he needed help bad.

But when he got to her house her mother's car wasn't there and Sharon was coming out the door ready to make a run for it which really pissed him off.

He grabbed her and she was scared, really scared, and he showed her the knife and told her she'd better not fucking scream or he'd cut her lying throat and then he dragged her into the dark back yard and ripped her blouse off and cut her tits a little bit with the knife and then he fucked her on the ground and she went wild and he said I love you I love you I love you, and she said she understood, she really did, they would work something out.

She said she'd go get some money for him, some food, wait here, and she ran in the house and he knew she was going to call the fucking cops because that's what women did. He didn't expect anything different.

He heard Sharon and her mother yelling at each other and then it was quiet, he figured they were hiding someplace from him. He went and sat on the porch-swing on the verandah and rocked it gently, really gently, just like when him and Sharon were kids. He was very quiet. God, he was good at this!

Then he saw the cop car coming down the street and he leapt off the porch and into the dark, the bushes, the shadows, not blaming her for calling the fucking cops because, what the fuck, he was dead meat and what could you do, eh?

48

Traps.

Sharon was jealous about her room; forbade her mother entry — and this was supposed to be *their* home. But the door hadn't been locked, had it? But what if Sharon were hiding — just waiting to leap out from someplace and shout at her mother, "Snoop! Snoop!"

But she pushed in. What did Sharon's anger matter now?

The room surprised her. She had expected the bed unmade, and clothes strewn on the floor, a pair of jeans flung sprawling in the corner or over a chair, odd socks, she expected a terrible mess, but the room was quite tidy. The bed was made. The picture in her mind of a dressing table littered with open bottles of lotion and creams and crumpled lipsticked kleenexes was false, too. The surface of the dressing table was clean. From the mirror above it Lorraine confronted herself angrily. "Fool!" said the image of herself.

Lorraine looked around the room again. Sharon was a cheat, she thought.

Traps.

Lorraine did not rush to the closet. But she thought she walked to it with purpose in her stride, and she was surprised to catch herself in the mirror and find that she was hesitant, tentative, fearful. What was she afraid of? Did she expect a grinning daughter to come shrieking out of the closet like a jack-in-the-box? Oh, the *triumph* of "Snoop! Snoop!"

When Sharon had begun to lock her room, Lorraine thought it was just a gesture of some sort, the kind one might expect from an adolescent daughter, and what she longed to do was talk to the other women at the hospital, women she worked with, about all their daughters, and trade stories back and forth, just talking daughters, being *normal*. Sharon would be typical, normal. But Lee had robbed her of that. Lee had let her think he was dead, and made it impossible for Lorraine to join in with the other women when they talked and laughed and said that of course *all girls* go through stages, you have to expect them. It was unfair. Life was supposed to be *normal*!

Angry now, Lorraine yanked open the closet door — and of course there was no Sharon screaming like a mad woman and of course the closet was just as she expected — shoes flung every which way on the floor, how would you find even a *pair*? And fallen wire coat hangers. Sharon couldn't be bothered to pick them up. And the clothes rack was stuffed so badly that everything wrinkled everything else, winter and summer clothes together in no order, and shoe boxes piled on the shelf almost to the ceiling. Where in the world did she get all these shoes? In a moment she discovered that many of the shoes had never been worn; they were still in their tissue paper.

She returned to the bedroom and pulled back the bedspread and covers from the bed. The sheets were dirty.

Traps.

She pulled open a drawer of the dresser — and found winter sweaters and summer blouses crumpled together. It made her furious. What did the girl think she was doing? Who did she think she was fooling? A yellow blouse which Lorraine had labored to iron carefully (there were pleats) — when? just last week — was stuffed wilfully and deliberately into a corner. It was a deliberate act of cruelty!

Under the yellow blouse were underpants; under the underpants were the letters. Lorraine was holding the crumpled yellow blouse in her hand with the divorce letter when she found the letters from Lee to Sharon. Stodd

Enterprises indeed. *Stodd* was a joke figure — a funny man Lee created to entertain Sharon when she was little and he thought her just adorable. He drew *Stodd* as a stick figure with green clothes. He had all sorts of adventures in parks and shops. Lee liked to tell Sharon a story and then take her to the very shop where he had set the story so the little Sharon could cry out, "Look — there's Mr. Stodd's tie!" and Lee would say, "Well, we'd better buy it then." And he would buy it and he would wear it. It was another way Lee managed to get just whatever it was he wanted.

The letters made her sick.

He had been alive all along, writing to her! The two of them deceiving her, having the laugh on her, mocking her. Stupid mother!

Then she found the deed to the house. Why did Sharon have the deed to the house? What were they going to do with her?

She flung the underclothes out of the drawer, she grabbed the sweaters and blouses and threw them on the floor, she yanked the bedding off the bed and threw it out the door — then kicked the clothes down the stairs.

My darling girl! Oh!

49

Now she had the girl, she had Proof, Proof! Letters from Toronto, letter from a lawyer, the deed, the yellow blouse. What do you have to say about this, young lady?!

Sharon was running up the stairs half-naked.

"He cut me, he cut me! Mother!"

"What do you have to say about this, young lady?"

"Mother! He cut me, he raped me, call the police, Mother. Mother!"

"You little liar!"

"Mother! He *cut* Me! He *cut* Me! Look!"

"You little liar!"

Her mother rushed at her.

"It's not my fault. Mother! Not my fault! Mother *stop*!"

Lorraine was slapping at her with her fists, swatting at her with the letters in her hand, the blouse.

"Mother!"

"Little liar!"

"Look, look, look. He cut me! Look! He did!"

Her mother pushed her hard. Her mother's teeth were gritted.

"*It's not my fault!*" screamed Sharon.

Her mother pushed her hard and Sharon fell backwards and smashed her head against the newel post. There was an explosion of color in her head and then nothing.

50

Lorraine thought, Good enough for her, Good enough for her.

Lorraine walked away. She refused to think about her any more. She would not think about her, the little liar. What she had to do was get rid of those disgusting letters. She got them and stepped over Sharon at the top of the stairs and went downstairs to the kitchen, put the letters in a plastic bag from the grocery and put them behind the pots and pans on the lower shelf where nobody would ever find them, proof of treachery. Sharon. Good enough for her.

But she thought she had better dial 911. She did. She said Emergency and gave her address and hung up. Let them deal with it. She would not tell anybody anything.

In a few moments she heard the sirens coming down the hill. They were police sirens, not ambulance sirens. What had she said to 911? She didn't care. The sirens were cut off, they did that when they got close. She heard the porch-swing on the verandah bump against the house. She didn't care. She wondered if she would start to weep but she didn't feel like it now. She felt like stale bread. She didn't care. Stale bread.

Stringy leapt off the porch barefoot, started running. He expected to be gunned down from behind. That's the way things were. You ran because that, too, was the way things were: you did what you had to do. He was barefoot and naked to the waist except for the tattoos and his cock was hanging out of his pants because it felt right to sit on the swing on Sharon's verandah with his cock out and barefoot and bare-chested (O his beautiful tattoos), waiting for the cops while she was inside crying to her mother and calling the cops. When he heard the sirens on the hill he knew they were coming for him and when he saw the cop car turn the corner, sirens off and no signal lights flashing, he knew it was his turn and he leapt off the porch, started running. The headlights of the cop car caught him and he expected to be shot down chasing his shadow because that's the way things are, but that didn't happen. One of the cops yelled "Hey!" and then again "Hey!" but Stringy was running across some guy's wet lawn squishing and slipping and then on concrete hurting his feet (his weight pounded down; the concrete tore at the soles of his feet), then on dirt, through bushes scratching himself (that, too, was appropriate), more lawns, more hedges, it became a rhythm until he achieved a kind of darkness which distance gives, and space. He was nearly to the river when he heard more sirens on the hill. They belonged to him, too. He made it to his hiding place, curled up and tried to get warm, but he couldn't. Cold. Cold. Cold. Why was he always so fucking *cold*?

52

The Mother didn't answer the door but the door was open
so we went in and saw the mess on the stairs and her sitting
in the living room staring into space. The first assumption
was robbery — because she was acting the way people do
when they've been robbed, they can't believe it, can't
believe somebody would intrude into their private lives like
this — and because of the mess. You take a kid from the
Irishtown Road and when he gets some drugs in him, he
goes out to rob — for money, of course, but for the
vengeance, too: he wants revenge on all the god-damned
people who have it better than he does. He wants revenge
for being the stupid shit he is — so he trashes the place.
Sometimes a kid like that will shit someplace — on the
couch maybe. So the first thing I did was sniff for shit. But
maybe there wasn't time; maybe Mrs. Branaman's return
interrupted him.

Then Bill went upstairs and called back: "It's up here."

Jesus. She had to sit there and listen to that: "It's up
here."

Mothers and daughters — sometimes they get so close,
especially after something happens like a father running
out on them. They get to be more like sisters than like
mother and daughter. Each becomes the other's reason for
living. You see that around here quite a bit: two women
getting old, one old and the other older, shuffling around
a big house, losing their minds.

Now this. "It's up here." Jesus.

53

Berry and Johnson almost got the kid right then, you know. They were driving down University Avenue towards the underpass and they see this running figure coming towards them, just high-tailing it. Well, you can tell, even at a distance, the run of somebody out of control and this guy was out of control. His arms were going every which way and his hair was flying. He wasn't wearing anything but a pair of jeans. They saw that he was tattooed, although they couldn't make out what the tattoos were. Johnson yelled out the window to the kid to Hold It Right There, but of course he didn't, and by the time they got turned around the kid was gone in the backyards of the neighborhood. We got a couple of calls within minutes about this guy running through backyards, but there was nothing we could do but cruise around the neighborhood with the spotlight. You can't surround a neighborhood without an army, and even if you could, what you'd invoke would be a violent response. Experienced police procedure is to wait and pick him up in the open if at all possible. When you corner a crazy you're asking for violence. The rule is: Give 'Em Room To Give Themselves Up. But he slipped away in the dark. Then we got the message to come help out at the Branaman residence, they had a bad one.

The spotlights — Jesus! They freak people. We had three cars with spotlights cruising around and they were shooting lights into hedges and up the sides of houses (don't ask me what for), and what they got were frightened faces and people yelling out windows to ask just what was going on. So then they had to stop to tell people to stay inside and lock their doors — and the people rushed off to make sure everything was locked up — and then they came back to the windows: "Hey, what's going *on*?"

"It's all right, nothing to worry about."

So after a while Kennedy comes by and says turn the fucking lights off, he's gone. So we did.

But by now everybody was awake and telephoning one another. They'd spotted the police cars in front of the Branaman place and the ambulance and sure enough in a few minutes one, then two, then three or four officious sorts came wandering by "to see if they could help." Shit. What they wanted was to watch TV live. The TV boys were there pretty quick, too, so we had the whole circus — taking the body out the front door and down the steps to be seen on the six o'clock news tomorrow. They'd all be watching that for sure.

All right, we said, all right, the story's over. Go home. Go back to bed. And we turned off all but one of the lights in the house and everybody left but Jim Dandy and one of our girls. They stayed to try to talk to the mother. She had frozen right up, understandably enough. When things happen worse than you can imagine you freeze right up. She couldn't even tell them if there was a friend or clergyman they could call. So they sat with her until our girl went out and got a neighbor woman who said of course she'd be glad to help out but she really didn't know the Branamans, nobody did since the husband ran away ten years ago.

55

See — at this point we didn't have any idea that we were dealing with the same guy who tried to rob the bank. We didn't begin to put that together until we brought the physical evidence downtown. What he'd left behind on the porch were his K-Mart running shoes, a Harley-Davidson T-shirt, and a Rambo knife — the weapon of choice for crazies these days. So we could put the story together pretty clearly from the physical evidence alone, and when we found out that she'd been cut on the breasts we figured that he had tortured her before he raped and killed her. Then Jim Dandy saw the Harley-Davidson T-shirt and said that's what the guy was wearing who tried to rob the bank — and Sharon Branaman worked in that bank. Whoa, we said, there's a personal connection. Bingo.

56

Berry and Johnson picked him up. No big deal. They were driving their cruiser along the road by the railway cut near the university and they spotted Stringy Keeler walking on the railway ties, head down, half-naked. They drove to where the road crossed the tracks and parked the car maybe 25 yards away, out of sight, and waited for Stringy to show up. When he did, Berry said, "Hey, come here Stringy. Come on." Stringy just walked up and joined them. Surprising? No, not really. That's the way things usually happen in a place like this. You usually know who did it and you just go get him. Those stand-off things are strictly for TV. We've had the SWAT team out three times this past year just so they can wear their neat black baseball caps and play TV. Everybody likes to play TV. The first time there was a drunk guy beating his wife and somebody thought they saw a gun and heard a gunshot. After we got the guy nobody would admit saying there was a gun or a gunshot. The second time there was this crazy kid in army clothes with a replica gun trying to scare his buddy. He was playing TV; so we played TV in response. The third time there was a drunk soldier on the roof of the legislature. He was unarmed — but hey, you have to take this stuff seriously sometimes, especially after Lortie, eh? And who doesn't think about shooting a politician now and then?

57

When Lee came back she wasn't expecting him and didn't care. He walked in the house big as you please and blubbered about Sharon, saying how terrible this was, he should never have left, and so on. He sat in the wicker chair by the front window and blubbered. He wanted me to hear him. He wanted me to feel sorry for him because his beloved daughter had died. He wanted to make a show of himself.

He said he was moving into Sharon's room and I didn't say anything. I expecting nothing other. He is probably looking for the deed. Let him sleep in her bed, see if I care!

58

The father was something else. We thought the guy was crippled. He limped all the time, like he had a war injury or something, but somebody noticed it was sometimes one leg and sometimes the other. He came into the station to say that after he struck the boy in the classroom he fled because he should not have hit the boy; it had ruined his career and driven him half-mad. But he had been right, hadn't he? The kid was a killer, he said. He knew that from the beginning.

59

Everybody wants a piece of you, you're fucking public property. Fucking cops get a hoot out of the tattoos. They've heard about them they say, like a fucking zoo. They drag my ass all over the place, sit here, sit there, where you been, this here's your lawyer, a fat lady who looks worried. The detective who handled me was Jim Dandy. I knew him from before. Everybody knows fucking Jim Dandy. He's got wavy hair, wears a ring, talks at you all the time, says he is interrogating you but is really fucking talking to himself in front of you, tells stories about how hard it was on the fucking farm where his old man used to take a logging chain to him, now what about old Gibby? I say nothing because that is just what fucking Gibby is to me. *Nothing* I say when nothing ain't enough and they don't believe that either. Fucking cops want the answers they want and its no use *what* you fucking say or don't say it has to fit what they want to put in the fucking file-folders. I did not kill Sharon I tell my fat lawyer, I did not kill Sharon I tell Jim Dandy, I don't know what you are fucking talking about man and he says don't say fuck because it will offend Mrs. Bettinger who is taking notes, then he goes off to get a Coke which he thinks is a big favor to me and I take off my shirt because its hot and what the fuck more can they do to me? Jim Dandy comes back and sees Mrs. Bettinger back up against the wall and goes snaky yelling at me and I say what the hell did I do? and he says your scaring Mrs. Bettinger and I say I didn't even notice, I was hot, I say, and he is really pissed off about that, I am supposed to apologize to her, so I do, what the fuck do I care? I put my shirt back on, he goes thoughtful and says

maybe the tattoos made me do it, tattoos have influence on
me, were they a club practice or something? I don't know
what the hell he is talking about and *then* he says he is not
interrogating me just talking, do I want a shower? This
Mrs. Bettinger says I can certainly use one and she's right.
I want a shower and I want to sleep. All I want to do is
sleep, sleep, so my fat lawyer Mrs. McCrory says she'll ask
for a psychological assessment and I say what for I didn't
do it but she just goes on and on and I say what the fuck
do I have to do to get you to believe I didn't do it and she
says okay okay and I tell her alright I did do it, fuck her,
fuck everybody and I tell Jim Dandy that too and he's not
satisfied with that either. We go to court it's all solemn, the
judge wears robes the lawyers wear robes all of them like
fucking birds, and the Mounties are there looking perfectly
fucking splendid in their red coats and shiny boots what
were they there for? But the judge talks like it's everyday
and that pisses me off because I think shit, he's going to
send me to jail where I am going to get fucking killed and
he's talking like it's just everyday. It goes on and on — cops
appear, talk, disappear. Jim Dandy sits on the bench in
front, Mrs. McCrory doesn't even look at me, asks questions of the fucking cops, gives in every time. She says she
is not going to put me on the stand. Okay. She says we're
dealing just with physical evidence now. They have
Sharon's clothes, even her panties. Mrs. McCrory says they
are going to try to show I raped and tortured her but deny
cutting her. Mrs. McCrory is a nice lady who tells me she
knows I've had a hard life and she's trying to do her best
for me but I have to co-operate and I tell her I am fucking
co-operating but I don't know what fucking answers she
wants. Did I have a knife? You know I did. Where did I get
it? From Match. Where is Match? Fuck, I don't know,
probably dead — and she goes despairing like she thinks I
have killed Match and dumped his body in the woods

somewhere and fuck, I think, what a good idea, the sonofa-bitch didn't bring me the Big Mac he promised. You get killed for things like that in prison, Match, you know the fucking rules. So I say to Mrs. McCrory, yeah, I killed Match and she says Stringy your not telling the truth and I say what do you want, the truth or what you want to hear and she says this sounds desperate to me.

Well fuck what can I say?

Who killed Sharon?

I didn't even know she was dead until Jim Dandy told me, and O shit that was a twist. Twisted right through me, hurt like hell, bent me right over but I didn't yell, you can't *ever* give the fuckers the satisfaction, so I said, yeah? He said it wasn't going to be hard to connect me with her. She was full of semen he says, and that stuff is like a fingerprint otherwise kids could look like anybody, eh? not their parents.

Fucking wise guy is Jim Dandy. I tell him her fucking father did it. You should see that sonofabitch in court. Sits there holding Sharon's mother's hand, what an asshole, a really disgusting piece of shit. I told Jim Dandy and Mrs. McCrory both that it was Sharon's father who took the ruler to me when I was in Grade Seven and I tell them about the metal edge and say look, I still have the scars and its fucking true! Jim Dandy writes that down, Mrs. McCrory writes that down. That's not especially good, she says to me. Motive, she says. Revenge. Why would I want revenge on that piece of shit I say. Maybe you didn't know you wanted it she says and I tell her she's jerking me around, don't. Look, I say, Sharon came *after* me. She came up to me in the Mall and she laid her tits right out there for me and we went to the gravel pit two, three days later and she went right down on me, pulled it out of my pants, she wanted me. She liked my tattoos, thought they were great. Stringy, Jim Dandy says, you're pitiful. Fuck you too I say.

Then the judge gets after me for tipping back my fucking chair. Jesus! I didn't even know I was doing it, had no idea what he was on about, he's looking hard at me and the old guy the bailiff is repeating what he said to me. I'm supposed to pay attention to all this shit they are saying about me but they have no intention of believing what I say. How could her father have done it they say to me, he wasn't even here, he was in Toronto. How do you know that, I say, he was hiding in the fucking attic. Stringy, says Jim Dandy, you're pitiful. He thinks he's being fucking kind. Don't do me no favors, I tell him. Mrs. McCrory says she wants to do what's best for me. I tell her she's going to get me killed, that's what she's going to do. What's going to happen is the Suit is going to let out word that I informed on somebody.

But you didn't, she says.

That's why he's going to say it, I explain, and if I'm found guilty of this fucking crime it gives them a chance to kill me in prison.

Who?

Them, how the hell do I know? I don't even know who Suit is working for. Cops.

We won't let that happen, she says, and I say thanks but she's got no influence whatever in prison, there's nothing she can do to stop it. Why would I want to kill Sharon, I say, I loved her. Fuck, I loved making love to her. She was great. She was sweet. Why would I want to kill her, why the fuck won't anybody believe me. She says I used my knife on her and I say that doesn't mean I didn't love her. Women like that kind of stuff I say and she says O Stringy. How the fuck did I get a woman lawyer? Court-appointed. No offense, I say, but shit. Do you want another lawyer? No I say, shit — I like you, I say, you just won't fucking *believe me*. She says she's trying, she really is, and I believe that. But don't fall asleep in court, she says, and don't tip my chair back. The judge thinks that is showing disrespect, and maybe I can keep my snake hand not prominently displayed. People kill people for love, she says like its an explanation. Fuck I say. You know that, she says, from prison. There were guys in prison who killed people they loved weren't there? No I say, guys in prison killed their old ladies because their old ladies were jerking them around or cheating on them. What do you mean by that? Fucked somebody else or ran out on them, that kind of thing. Stringy, she says, people don't kill because of the other person but because of themselves. Shit, I say. How does she know about that, whatever it is. I know, she says, I'm not so naive as you think. What do you mean naive? She wrote the word for me like a teacher. Now I know it, you notice. That doesn't make any fucking sense, I say. Not everything does, she says. Well fuck, I say, and she laughs. She thinks she understands things because she's a Catholic mother even though she's divorced now. She asks me if I'm Catholic. No, I'm not, I say. Do I have to confess to that too? She laughs Stringy, Stringy, Stringy. Jesus H. Fucking Christ, I say, I am going to get *killed*, this is not funny. She's pissed off that I'm not laughing so she says There's No Death Penalty. That's what you think, I say, they got guys to kill you in prison — because there's no fucking shortage of killers in prison, I say. Pay attention, I tell her. I think she's about to cry so I apologize and then she apologizes to me and O shit, this is getting to be too fucking much. That's okay Stringy she says, everything's going to be okay, was she going to leave you? Caught me off-guard, shit. Can't trust anybody. Slipped right in there. Yeah she was going to leave me. I hit her. Mrs. McCrory nods — does that mean good or bad I say. You didn't want her to go? Fuck no! Why not? She was my lady. You owned her? Shit, she was my lady. Stringy she says you can't own somebody. What is this, some kind of women's lib shit? I say. You love somebody you own her, that's the way it is. O dear she says,

O dear. I loved her so I'm not going to kill her, okay? Unless she tries to leave, she says. I just hit her, that's not killing her. All right, she says. You don't believe that, do you? I say. Well, she says, one thing leads to another. Fuck they do, I say.

Why did you rob the bank, she says. To show her, I said, so she wouldn't leave. I figured I'd show her how much I cared and she wouldn't leave.

In court Mrs. McCrory doesn't say any of this but I'm not paying too much attention. Trying to sit up straight and sleep with my eyes open. Willie Jay said he could do that and I think it's a good thing to learn, I don't want the judge saying again this is not school young man you sit up straight in a court of law. Fucking look on Branaman's face says I Told You So. I mouth at him that he's the one I wish I killed and all of a sudden people are running all over the fucking place and I'm looking around wondering what the fuck is happening, what's going on.

Mrs. McCrory says don't say anything, don't say anything and I'm saying okay, okay, okay. God what a madhouse. The jury is sent out and the judge is talking to counsel and I'm hustled back to the room off the courtroom where the old guy the bailiff asks if I want a Coke? Anything in it? I ask. What do you mean? he says. What the fuck good is a Coke with nothing in it, I say. He looks away. I wave the snake head at him and laugh and he thinks I'm nuts, of course. Mrs. McCrory says the psychological assessment says I'm sane and I say fuck yeah I am, it's just that I'm fucking boxed.

Sun's out. Feels good. I feel pretty good until I have to go sit in court and everybody is staring at me thinking and I'm thinking that I am going to be killed and it will hurt worse than anybody can know. They don't want you to escape the pain. If she really wants to help me I tell Mrs. McCrory, get me some drugs so I can overdose and that will cause real shit because there's always drugs in prison but nobody knows about it until somebody overdoses. Mrs. McCrory looks knowing as hell and says she's learning a lot from me, she came to the Law late in life after her ex-husband said she was drinking too much. She was she says so she went to law school for something to do. Shit I say I'm being defended by somebody who does this for a hobby! Hey, I shout, get me a real lawyer! Stringy, she says, I know my stuff and I'm doing my best for you. I like to tease her, I say. O Stringy, you really did love her didn't you. More 'n I can say, I say. There's a country song that says it right, but I can't remember it. I'm no good at music. Willie Jay said he could play the guitar, he used to finger a broom like it was a guitar and fool around, hell I wouldn't have known if he was lying about that too or not. I'd like to have seen his face if I told him about Sharon, what a great fuck she was and what a great set of tits she had and how she could make me go fucking blind so there was nothing else in the world, nothing but sweet nothing.

Life was so sweet.
You don't hear the beat.

How's that. I'm a poet. I showed that to Mrs. McCrory and she said Stringy you ought to be a writer. Well I said I can spell *naive* and she says I'm more than half way there then. What I expect sometimes is that Sharon is going to walk into the courtroom and everything is going to be cleared up okay and Old Branaman is going to shit his pants. I open my eyes, but she's not there. I dream about her at night, too, not just her tits and cunt, Mrs. McCrory, but all the sweet things about her — she was so nice, so quality, she was so fucking lonely, you know? She was the loneliest person I ever met. She liked me to be mean so I was. She wanted tough, eh, and I wanted sweet. Okay? Sharon was sweet. Like eating a peach. Those nice tits of hers, they weren't big but not small either, bigger than a peach though. We were both naked out at the gravel pit one day and I had some peaches and we ate them naked and the juice dripped on her arm and on her tits and I licked it off her and she licked me. How's that? Is that love or what?

60

Stringy pulled the rug out from under Lynn McCrory. Everything that could go wrong, did. No, that's not quite fair. The case had been at best a delicate construction. The Crown brought in a charge of First Degree Murder (a charge which she thought was most certainly arguable) because the murder was committed in the course of a sexual assault (not the semen as evidence, but the knife, the knife wounds), and in the case of a murder committed in the course of sexual assault, a charge of First Degree Murder was obligatory. I argued that my client denied having raped or wounded the girl, and there were no witnesses. But we came out of the Preliminary with the charge intact; and that's how we went to trial.

I was not, however, quite so unhappy as I might have been — despite Stringy's recalcitrance, and his awkward willingness to say whatever he thought I wanted him to say. What I hoped would happen is that the Crown would realize that, without a witness, their case would — if not exactly collapse — become pretty thin, and they would agree to a reduction of the charge to Second Degree (a crime of passion), and then all I had to do was sell that to Stringy, and all would be — if not well — better than otherwise.

We might take that as a general principle of life.

What I wanted for Stringy was a sentence *other* than twenty-five years with no parole — which he would have received if he were convicted of First Degree Murder. What I was trying to get for him was parole in ten years. The truth is that I thought the Crown had over-extended themselves — fooled by Stringy's tattoos, perhaps, into thinking they had a born criminal here or a crazy, or by the fact that they were faced by a chubby woman defence lawyer whose hair was beginning to go grey — who has a dangerous tendency to care too much about her clients. Blame my Catholic upbringing. Blame the nuns. I do. I blame them for all sorts of things.

But where their case was weakest was where I was attacking it. They had no physical evidence to place Stringy at the scene of the crime — that is, upstairs in the Branaman house. If you do not have a witness, your physical evidence had better be impeccable.

But there was no sign of blood in Sharon's room, nor on the stairs.

There were none of Stringy's pubic hairs in the room. On Sharon's body, yes (but he admitted they had sexual intercourse; he insisted they were lovers — an assertion discounted by the Crown because there were no witnesses who had ever seen them together — I couldn't find any either), but none in the room, on or in the bed, on the floor. In truth, I believe the police forgot to check. Still, it was an absence of something which might have been expected, and I went after the policeman in charge — a prissy fellow named Winslow — vigorously. Jim Dandy, seated on the front row of courtroom benches behind me, squirmed.

But all of that was just to set them up for the one piece of evidence they badly needed and did not have: fingerprints. There were *no* fingerprints of Stringy in Sharon's bedroom or on the stairway banisters or anywhere in the house. Not one.

So, if he tortured, raped, and killed her — you might say — it had to have been done somewhere else.

But you might argue that he could have dragged her half-naked body inside and dumped her at the top of the stairs, where Mrs. Branaman found her.

If so, wouldn't there have been fingerprints?

Why the mess upstairs, then?

Somebody else, I said. Person or persons unknown.

I think I had them thinking. Mrs. Branaman was on the stand at that point, and she was a deeply depressed woman. She had come home and found Sharon's clothes strewn all over and Sharon, her daughter, dead. Mrs. Branaman was all but comatose. She had great difficulty speaking. She didn't understand what I was talking about, she said. I asked if there were boy-friends.

No.

Did Sharon sneak out, did she conceal, perhaps, a relationship from her mother?

She perked right up at that. No! said Mrs. Branaman. She would have known! She and her daughter were *friends*!

And at that moment Stringy — who had clearly not been paying one whit of attention — stood up in the prisoner's dock and said: "O what the fuck, let's get this crap over with, I did it — okay?"

O my God.

The court was stunned into silence. No — more than that. Immobility. No one moved.

Stringy had apparently not anticipated this response.

Okay? he said. Okay?

He looked around helpfully.

And then of course we all came back to life. The bailiff moved towards Stringy to get him to sit down (which he was already doing), and the judge glared — first at Stringy, for messing up the order of his court (and Judge McKinnon is very particular about the order in his court), and then at me. I admit it; I slumped into my chair. O despair — the ultimate sin.

Counsel were beckoned to the bench. Recess was declared. The accused was taken out. The jury filed out. Crown prosecutor and I met with the judge. I was scolded for my inability to control my client and saw that I was being blamed, too, for the failings of all women lawyers and all women, too, while he was at it.

And we found ourselves at a tricky point. It was a delicate situation and I was not exactly emotionally prepared for it. The Crown realized that their case was slipping away from them, and so this was an opportunity to say, okay — we'll agree to Second Degree. But by confessing while he was still charged with First Degree, hadn't Stringy put himself in a box — that particular box of First Degree Murder? Could we get a reduction at this point? Had he not confessed to First Degree?

Well of course not, I said. He had *admitted guilt*. That was a long way from a *confession*. They had *not* proved anything, I said, except what we admitted: that he had intercourse with the girl, and now he said he "did it." So he might be guilty, but they were damned well going to have to *prove* that sexual *assault*!

Okay. Okay. Okay.

We agreed: Second Degree.

And was Stringy happy? Was he pleased that I had done what a good criminal lawyer does — the *best possible*? Not a bit of it.

He said he didn't care whether it was First or Second Degree. By sending him to jail I was sending him to a grave. Worse, he said, the fuckers would make sure he suffered.

61

You know what the silly little fuck did? He turned up at sentencing with his girl friend's name carved into his forehead. Oh, there was shit to pay for that. He'd done it with a pair of nail-clippers and then covered it with a rag, so he goes into court looking like a gypsy or something. Questions are going to be asked about who let him do the carving and where'd he get the rag and shit like that. I'll get blamed. I don't really give a fuck. The poor little shit is in for a hard time, especially if the Bikers are after him for some reason. So he gets into court and yanks off the rag and there is S H A R O N across his forehead in scabby blood. Looked like he'd been ripped with barbed-wire, which is a Biker trick. The judge was some pissed off. What a zoo. He gives Stringy fifteen years before parole. He could have given him as little as ten.

Trying to cheer him up a little afterwards, I ask him about those damned tattoos. Doesn't he ever get tired of them, I ask. I thought it would be like watching the same TV program forever. No channel changes allowed.

But he was too down to say anything. He thought he was dead.

62

Afterwards?

Lorraine reached a settlement with the hospital. She insisted she was dying of cancer, although tests showed no indication of the illness. It was clear, however, that she was suffering from a psychiatric problem, probably as the result of her daughter's murder, and everyone did their best to be sympathetic and understanding. Clearly, she could not continue employment, although she insisted she could. An agreement for long-term disability leave at reduced pay until retirement was proposed, and her lawyer accepted the deal, although she was unhappy with the arrangement.

The house is obviously in bad repair. It hasn't been painted since god knows when, and it shows. The clapboards are grey, the verandah is sagging, and the steps are rotting. The shades are always pulled down, and small children run past holding one another's hands, telling stories about the old witch who lives there with the old man. Leaves pile up on the front lawn; soggy advertising flyers are left to dissolve into pulp. The city has sent clean-up notices, but all have been ignored, and the city officials seem unwilling or unable to press for action.

He is seen sometimes on the street on his way to or from the liquor store, but she is seen rarely. On one occasion, however, she fell on the ice, and an ambulance was called and she was brought, protesting, to the hospital.

Do you know what they found? They found she was wearing an aluminum pie pan in her underwear. "For the Cancer," she said. She insisted on it being returned to her.